HIDDEN IN AMISH COUNTRY

DANA R. LYNN

HARLEQUIN® LOVE INSPIRED® SUSPENSE

Recycling programs
for this product may
not exist in your area.

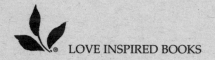 LOVE INSPIRED BOOKS

ISBN-13: 978-1-335-23238-0

Hidden in Amish Country

www.Harlequin.com

Printed in U.S.A.

"I can't stay here."

Ben glanced to see that Sadie had moved to his side. "You want to leave?"

"I have to, Ben. I think that my memories are starting to come back to me. And I am desperate to keep trying to find Kurt. If the police hide me away somewhere, my hands are tied. I'd be alone and helpless, with no way to find the truth."

"Then we will keep moving toward where my family is."

"You still want to go with me? What if I bring danger to your family?"

"Sadie, I was honest when I said I think my old district is the safest place for you. We must trust in *Gott*. He will protect us."

However, Ben couldn't quite shake the worry that Mason Green was still out there. Nor could he forget the flashbacks that Sadie was experiencing.

What if the amnesia she was afflicted with hid a dark secret? One that could hurt her as much as Mason Green could?

How was he to protect her and his family from a danger that she couldn't remember?

Dana R. Lynn grew up in Illinois. She met her husband at a wedding and told her parents she'd met the man she was going to marry. Nineteen months later, they were married. Today, they live in rural northwestern Pennsylvania with enough animals to start a petting zoo. In addition to writing, she works as a teacher for the deaf and hard of hearing and works in several ministries in her church.

Books by Dana R. Lynn

Love Inspired Suspense

Amish Country Justice

Amish Witness Protection

Visit the Author Profile page at Harlequin.com.

Fear thou not; for I am with thee: be not dismayed;
for I am thy God: I will strengthen thee;
yea, I will help thee; yea, I will uphold thee
with the right hand of my righteousness.
—Isaiah 41:10

To my husband, Brad. Even after so many years, you are still my best friend and the love of my life.

ONE

Someone was watching her.

Sadie Standings whipped her head around so fast that her light brown hair swung across her face, blocking her vision. Shoving her fingers through her hair to push it out of the way, she searched the area behind her. The parking lot at the local shopping mall was busy, filled with people who had stopped on their way home from work, but none of the other shoppers appeared to be looking in her direction. Seeing no one suspicious, she scrunched her eyes into a squint, desperately trying to catch sight of whoever was watching her. Still, she saw nothing.

She should have been comforted.

She wasn't. Unease still pricked at her.

Despite all evidence to the contrary, she knew that she was under surveillance. In fact, she had known since the day before when she had spotted the man with the cold blue eyes watching her as she left the post office. He was so familiar. When she had seen him, she had a flash of what she thought may have been a memory, but it had made no sense. In her mind, she could hear a cold voice calling to her, shouting, but couldn't make out the words. Was it a threat? A warning? Although she couldn't understand the words, the tone was harsh.

Although it seemed improbable, she knew that she had seen him somewhere before and instinctively cringed. A chill had run through her when his posture stiffened at her reaction. Had she offended him? She didn't think so. Since then, she'd had the sensation of hard eyes boring into her. It was like walking around with a target on her back, like the one her brother used when sighting in his rifle before hunting season.

The spot between her shoulder blades tingled again, like a spider skittering across her skin. He was there. Somewhere he was out there, watching her. Briefly, the idea of going to the police crossed her mind, but she quickly vetoed it. What would she tell them? That she believed someone she'd bumped into was following her, but she hadn't actually *seen* him following her? Oh, and she thought she might have met him before, but had no real recollection of doing so. Yeah, right. They'd think she was crazy or making the story up.

Thankfully, she was in a parking lot full of other shoppers, so there was little chance that anyone would come after her. Still, she didn't like the feeling of being out in the open. Hoisting her purse higher on her shoulder, she held the bag close to her body and pushed herself to move faster. The October wind bit into her skin as she practically ran the last few feet to her car. Her eyes teared at the cold. She didn't care what the people around her thought. Every instinct inside her was screaming at her to flee.

She held out the key fob and pressed the unlock button several times as she approached her vehicle. The lights flashed in two short bursts. Opening the driver's side door, she threw herself inside. Her elbow slammed into the steering wheel in her haste. She ignored the sharp pain that shot down her arm. She pushed the key into the ignition with fingers that shook. The first time she tried to turn the key, it was stuck and wouldn't move. Not now. She'd had trouble with the ignition jamming before. Thoughts of being stranded here while someone with malicious intent drew closer crowded into her mind. Clenching her teeth, she held her breath and turned the steering wheel to the left. When it clicked, she tried to turn the key again.

Relief flooded through her as the engine roared to life. The sooner she arrived home and was locked inside her house, the better she'd feel. She was concerned that someone might try to break into her house, but she shoved that fear aside. She had good locks, and she didn't live alone in the house her family had owned for the past fifteen years. Her brother would be home shortly.

Pulling out of the parking lot, she sighed, allowing the tension that had built up inside her to drain away. She had half-expected someone to follow her, but no one did. Maybe she was being paranoid.

Suddenly her confidence that she had recognized the man dwindled. He probably just had one of those faces that looked vaguely like someone she had known. Even with the doubt, she couldn't completely shake the sensation that she had escaped from some nebulous danger.

She was being ridiculous.

She neared the intersection. Wow. She needed to pay attention to where she was going. She hadn't realized that she had driven so far already. She tapped the brake to slow as she neared the stop sign.

Her car didn't slow. Her insides quivered.

She pushed harder on the brake. In horror, she glanced down to see that her foot was all the way to the floorboard.

Her brakes weren't working.

The car stopped to the left started into the intersection. She was going to wreck! Slamming the heel of her hand against the horn, she let out three sharp blasts. The driver jerked to a halt, yelling angrily as Sadie vroomed past.

She held the steering wheel in a white-knuckled grip and leaned forward, her eyes frantically searching the passing roads.

In less than a mile, she'd be at another busy intersection. How far could she travel before she collided with someone? Making a split decision, she wrenched the wheel to the side and peeled off onto a dirt road. The road was at a slight incline. Her stomach began to settle as the vehicle started to slow as it continued uphill.

The relief vanished when she realized that on the other side of the incline was a steep drop. Her mouth was dry. The moment she crested that hill, her car would begin to accelerate again.

Frantically, she stomped on the brake, hoping against

all logic that the brake would suddenly begin to work again.

It didn't. As she neared the top, she knew with utter clarity that if she didn't figure out a way to stop the car, she was going to crash and possibly kill herself and anyone in her path.

"*Dat*, they're going to crash!"

Ben Mast heard his son's shout a mere moment before he heard the roar of a vehicle approaching way too fast. Throwing his hammer down on his work bench, he rushed out of the brown log-sided structure and raced down the gravel driveway to his seven-year-old son Nathaniel's side.

The red compact car swerved wildly down the hill, tires spinning on the slick surface.

Ben grabbed Nathaniel and dragged him back from the road, despite the boy's protests. If the driver left the road, he didn't want his son to become a victim of some *Englischer's* recklessness. His lips tightened in anger. Didn't these people care that others might be out on these roads? He knew for a fact there was a sign posted saying that children lived on this street.

The car zoomed past, the high-pitched whine of the engine searing the silent afternoon. He caught a glimpse of the driver's face and saw sheer panic. Why didn't she try to slow down?

A familiar clopping noise gained his attention. He whipped his head around, mouth so dry he couldn't have swallowed if he'd wanted to. A horse was coming up the hill. It was pulling a buggy with an Amish couple and several children. The man pulled on the reins, but the car was still coming. Where could the family go? Ben felt the inevitability of the collision clenching his stomach painfully.

"*Gott*, help them!" he shouted out.

The car swerved to the side, careening off the side of the road and plowing into an ancient maple tree with a horrendous crash. The tree shuddered, and the hood of the small car crunched in like it was made of cardboard. Steam burst from the engine, with a long, loud hiss.

There was no movement inside the car. Fearing the worst, Ben turned urgently to his son. "Go to Caleb and Lovina's," he said, pointing to the house across the street. "Caleb has a phone in his business office. Ask him to call for help."

Most of the houses on the road belonged to Amish families. Although there were a few *Englischer* homes, as well. Lovina and Caleb were their closest neighbors.

Nathaniel's head bobbed in a hurried nod, then he shot off across the street. Ben waited until he saw his son was with Lovina before he dashed down the street to the car. He knew that Caleb was probably already calling but giving Nathaniel a purpose would keep him out of harm's way. Ben reached the car and saw that the front windows had shattered upon impact. Glass crunched under his feet as he approached the driver's door.

"Miss?" The woman inside the car was hunched over the steering wheel, but he could see part of her face through the curtain of light brown hair. Blood was running down her cheek. Taking care not to cut his arm, he reached in through the broken window and placed his fingers on the side of her neck, feeling for a pulse. He found one. It was strong and steady. Ben sighed and closed his eyes, murmuring a soft prayer of thanksgiving.

The driver of the buggy stepped down to see if he could help. Ben heard the cries of children in the buggy. Looking up, he also saw that the woman sitting in the front looked very pregnant and quite ill.

"*Nee, denke.* Why don't you take your family home? My son went to Caleb's to call the ambulance."

The man nodded. "Once I get my wife and children home, I will come back to see if you need me."

Ben agreed, but his attention was back on the vehicle.

He looked at the front of the car and frowned. There was so much damage. He didn't see how she could have escaped injury; possibly she had internal bleeding. She'd have to go to the hospital. He flinched. He had lost his wife to a cancer that no one had been aware of until it was too late. Their unborn daughter had also perished. The hospital where they had died would forever be stamped in his memory. He never wanted to step inside one of those places again.

He looked again at the woman. It would be easier to decide what to do if the door weren't in the way. If it even opened. He looked doubtfully at how the frame had been bent on impact. He had to try it, though. To his surprise, he was able to wrench the door open. It swung wide and hung at an odd angle, but he was already focused on the occupant of the car. She was so still. He wished he could see her legs better. He wondered if he should try and pull her from the vehicle but decided against it. He didn't want to risk hurting her any more than she already was.

"Is she alive?" Caleb's deep voice startled him. He'd been so wrapped up in his inspection that he hadn't heard his neighbor approaching.

"*Jah*. I can't tell how bad she's hurt, but she's alive."

Caleb wrinkled up his nose. "What's that smell?"

Ben froze. The distinct sharp odor of gasoline rose to his nostrils. Bending down, he saw the gas was dripping from her car. She must have punctured the line during the crash. He reversed his earlier decision. She might have internal injuries, but if the car exploded, she'd be dead.

"Let's move her from the car," Ben said.

The other man grunted in response. Between the two of them, they slowly maneuvered the woman from the vehicle. Ben surveyed her for any other signs of damage as he helped Caleb carry her across the street to his porch. There was blood on her left arm, but other than that and the cut on her cheek, she appeared to be whole.

He looked around. Some of the neighbors had emerged from their houses to see what was happening. "Stay back," he yelled a warning. "There might be a gas leak."

Some of them stayed where they were, although several went back into their homes, shooing their children ahead of them.

Sirens sounded in the distance. As they zoomed closer, Nathaniel ran up to him and stared down at the woman.

"Is she going to die, *Dat*?" The little boy's voice trembled. It broke his heart to hear it. He wanted to say no, but he would never lie to his child. Nathaniel had already learned the hard truth of human frailty. Although Ben and his son did not speak of his wife's illness, he knew that Nathaniel had not forgotten the agony of watching his mother waste away and die. How could he forget it?

"I don't know, Nathaniel. It's in *Gott's* hands. We have called the ambulance, that's all we can do."

The ambulance arrived. Ben waved at them to pull up the driveway. A police car pulled up behind the accident, red and blue lights flashing. The paramedics jumped down from their vehicle and rushed to the young woman lying on the porch. With calm efficiency, they started checking her vital signs.

"You shouldn't move someone from a vehicle if you don't know the extent of their injuries," one of the paramedics informed Caleb and Ben.

Caleb grunted, unimpressed. Ben felt it was up to him to give an explanation.

"*Jah*, I know that. We smelled gasoline and feared it was too dangerous to leave her in the car."

He watched as they lifted the still-unconscious woman onto a stretcher. Something about her pale face surrounded by wavy light-brown hair tugged at him. Almost like a memory, but hazy. Hopefully they would find some identification in the car and be able to notify her next of kin. His mind again traveled to the hospital where he had spent the last day of his Lydia's life. It had seemed to him such a place should have been filled with warmth to comfort patients but was instead filled with *Englisch* technology. The idea of the stranger waking up alone in such a place bothered him, although he told himself that it wasn't his concern.

He had done his part. He had made sure the emergency personnel were called. She was being well cared for. If she had family, they would soon be with her.

It didn't help. What if she didn't have family?

He couldn't get the horrified expression on her face as she barreled down the hill out of his mind. Had she run into the tree on purpose to avoid the buggy?

The police were finishing up their inspection of the car. The tow truck arrived and hooked it up.

"Not that she'll be able to do anything with this," the driver remarked, chomping on a piece of gum. "I'm guessing the insurance adjuster will say it's a total loss."

"Why'd she crash? Did you see what happened?" an officer asked Ben.

He shook his head. "I saw her coming down the hill. It looked like she couldn't stop, but that's all I know."

The officers finished up, and within twenty minutes the street was quiet again.

But Ben remained unsettled. Something about the situation continued to eat at him.

"*Dat*. I found this." Nathaniel held up something for his father to inspect. It was a cell phone. Ben's brow furrowed. It had probably slipped from the woman's pocket when he and Caleb had carried her to the porch. The Amish didn't use cell phones, not even in their businesses. Their bishop allowed them to have a landline phone in their businesses if it was necessary, but cell phones were considered excessive. But from his interactions with them he knew that the *Englisch* relied heavily on their devices.

It gave him an excuse to check up on her, just to make sure she was all right. The thought made him pause. It wasn't like him to be so concerned about what was happening in the *Englisch* world. He had a few *Englisch* friends he'd made through his work as a carpenter, but he avoided any deep attachments. He had learned his lesson the hard way. He couldn't rely on others to protect his family. And technology couldn't always help. He had lost his wife and their unborn daughter when Lydia had been struck with cancer, and no amount of *Englisch* technology or medicine had been able to save them. All he had left was his son and he was determined to be careful.

He would check on her, he decided, then he would leave. His conscience would be eased, and he would never have to see the woman again.

His mind flashed back to the memory of the driver's panicked face before she had hit the tree. She had obviously been aware of the danger. He couldn't recall any of the telltale clues that she was trying to stop.

His eyes flashed to the tree in question. The bark had been scraped off in several places. He could see bits and pieces of it littering the ground. Although the mangled car was gone, he doubted he'd forget the image anytime soon.

Why hadn't she stopped?

TWO

"Sadie? Sadie, can you hear me?" a strange voice pleaded, over and over again.

Why wouldn't he just be quiet? Her head was pounding with every word he uttered. Irritated, she dragged her eyelids open to confront the man who kept talking to her when she just wanted to rest. Two blurry figures stood beside her bed. That didn't seem right. She blinked, and they wobbled before coalescing into one man. His messy brown hair and dark brown eyes gave her the impression of an excited puppy. He was obviously happy to see her.

But who was he?

Panic stirred inside her at the sudden realization that she had no memory of the man standing before her, a ridiculous grin stretched wide upon his face. He, however, obviously knew her.

"Who—who are you?" she gasped out, feeling like the panic was a steel band around her chest, making it difficult to take in a full breath of air.

His grin faltered and those brown eyes sharpened.

"Are you messing with me, Sadie?"

Sadie. The shock went through her. Her name was Sadie. The sound of the name was unfamiliar.

"My name is Sadie?"

The man's formerly grinning mouth was now a grim frown. His brow was furrowed. Concern emanated from him.

"Your name is Sadie Ann Standings," he began slowly, as if her ability to process information had disappeared along with her memory. She fought the urge to sigh in impatience. "My name is Kurt. Kurt Standings. I'm your brother."

She'd forgotten her own brother?

"You're my brother?" she blurted. She didn't doubt him, but it was so much to take in at once.

He shrugged. "Stepbrother, but our parents have been married since we were both eight years old. When they married, my dad adopted you, gave you our last name. That was sixteen years ago."

Which meant she was twenty-four. Why couldn't she remember any of this? He reached out a hand to touch her shoulder. She jerked it away from him, then winced at the hurt on his face. Still, she was relieved when he didn't try to touch her again. The thought of a stranger touching her so familiarly was disconcerting.

"Here," he said, pulling his wallet from his back pocket and drawing out a picture. A young woman with light brown hair and a younger version of the man standing before her stood behind an older couple sitting on a couch, smiling at the camera. She glanced at it and then back at him, awaiting the explanation. He jabbed a finger at the young woman. "That's you. This is your mom and my dad."

She looked closer and saw a clear resemblance between the two women.

"Where are our parents?" Shouldn't they have come the moment they heard she was in the hospital?

His face grew sober. "I'm sorry, Sadie. Dad and your mom, Hannah, were killed in a fire two years ago."

The loss swamped her, even though the people he talked about were strangers.

"What was your father's name?" she asked softly.

"Our father, Sadie. Your biological father was long gone. Our dad's name was Tim."

"Hannah and Tim," she whispered to herself, wishing she could remember.

"Look, we need to get the doctor in here." Kurt took the control near her bed and pressed the button.

Within minutes, a doctor and a nurse were in the room. The female doctor flashed a light in her eyes and asked her endless questions, most of which Sadie was unable to answer. She didn't recall her family, where she went to school, anything about her job. She couldn't even tell them what she had been doing when her car had crashed.

"You swerved to avoid colliding with an Amish buggy and hit a tree instead." The doctor lifted her eyes from her laptop and slid her glasses up to rest on the top of her head. "The car was totaled, or so I hear. You're very fortunate that no one else was hurt."

Sadie detected a faint note of censure in the doctor's voice but wasn't sure why.

"I guess." If only she could remember!

The doctor nodded. "You must have been going very fast to have hit the tree so hard."

"What about my memories? Will they come back?" This total blankness was intolerable. She couldn't imagine dealing with it for the rest of her life. A movement caught her attention. Kurt was frowning, his face disturbed. When he noticed her watching him, he smiled, but she could still see the strain in it.

The doctor's expression softened. "There's no way to know that. You may regain some memories, or you may regain all of them. In some instances, the amnesia is permanent. Your brother and your friends will undoubtedly be willing to help you fill in the missing memories."

"Of course, we will, sis. Don't you worry about it."

Which was silly. Obviously, she would worry about it. It was somewhat unsettling to have someone of whom she had no recollection talking to her with such familiarity. She wondered vaguely if they had been close siblings.

As the doctor was leaving, another stranger entered the room. Sadie felt her eyes widen. This stranger was taller than Kurt, and his dress was very simple. Blue button-down shirt, dark trousers, sturdy brown boots. His hair was dark, and so were his eyes. The lower part of his face was covered with a beard. No mustache, though. She blinked at the sight of an Amish man standing in her hospital room. The beard signified that he was married, or at least she thought it did. Huh. It struck her as odd that she could remember how the Amish dressed, but that she couldn't recall her own name.

"Ben!" Kurt strode to the door, astonishment stamped on his face. "What are you doing here?"

"Kurt. You know her?" He jerked the hand holding his hat toward where Sadie lay watching from the hospital bed. She could see the surprise in the rigidness of his posture.

"Know her? She's my sister." Kurt's voice retained its puzzlement.

Ben, whoever he was, hadn't said what he was doing there yet. Sadie listened avidly. Maybe he would have some details about what had happened to her. It was a rather desperate hope.

"Ah." Ben shifted. His eyes sought out Sadie. He blinked when he saw her watching him. A slow smile, that reminded her of a sunrise, took over his face. She'd been so focused on the beard that she hadn't noticed how gentle the deep brown eyes surrounded by several feathery laugh lines were. "It's *gut* to see you awake. You crashed in front of my house. My neighbor and I pulled you from the car. I found this after you were gone."

He pulled out a smartphone in a bright pink case and set it on the table beside her. It didn't look familiar, but then, nothing really did.

"Thank you for bringing it. And thanks also for helping me," she told him. "Do I know you?"

His thick eyebrows climbed up his forehead. "We've never met before."

She liked the way he talked, slow and soft.

Kurt stepped in before the silence could become uncomfortable. "She's got amnesia or something. Can't remember a thing. Her doctor popped in and said she may or may not remember everything."

That was a lot of information to be giving a stranger. Ben might know Kurt, but he had no true connection with her. She frowned at her brother, trying to let him know to stop telling his friend about her.

A knock sounded on the door. She sighed, wishing to be alone with her thoughts to sort out what she had learned. Kurt opened it. From her position on the bed she could make out a dark blue uniform and a gold badge. Finally. The police had arrived. Maybe she could get some answers. Kurt swung the door wider. "Hey, Keith. Do you have some news about my sister's accident?"

"Yes, as a matter of fact, I do." The officer entered the room.

Sadie sat up straighter. Kurt knew the officer, and the man hadn't said anything when he'd named her as his sister. Which meant she was, indeed, Kurt's stepsister. She noticed Kurt straightening his posture out of the corner of her eye as the officer approached her. She felt bad. To her, Kurt was someone she didn't know, but to him, she was his sister. If only she could remember!

"Keith? What caused my sister's accident?" Kurt's question brought her back to the present.

"There was a small jagged hole in the brake line. You most likely tore the line by going over rocks or rough terrain too fast. The line could have been slowly dripping for weeks without your being aware. You might have noticed your brakes feeling mushy. Too many people wait too long before getting their brakes fixed."

Kurt thanked the officer for his help. Sadie frowned. She had thought he would want to know what caused the accident, but she couldn't help noticing that his expression was even grimmer than before. His friend, Ben, seemed to notice something was wrong, as well.

"Kurt, are you well?"

Ben's voice was smooth and deep, unhurried with a slight accent. Not too noticeable, just somehow rounder than the speech she'd heard from others since she awoke.

Her brother glanced at her in a considering way. Then he apparently decided she needed to know what was going on.

"Sadie, you couldn't have had a leak for a long time." He drew in a deep breath. "You had the entire brake system, including the lines, replaced last week."

She shivered, though his meaning wasn't processing. "What are you trying to tell me?"

"This wasn't an accident."

"What do mean, it wasn't an accident?" Her voice came out strained, like she had to squeeze each and every painful word out.

Kurt—she couldn't think of him as her brother—gave her a look that was overflowing with sympathy. She was grateful he didn't attempt to touch her again.

"Someone tried to hurt you. Someone deliberately made it so that your car would run out of brake fluid while you were driving."

She shuddered. The fear and panic she had felt since awaking with no memory threatened to pull her under.

Already she could feel the blackness dragging her down. She fought her way through it. The doctor had said that her memories might return.

The other man, Ben, shifted beside the bed. "If you feel your sister was in danger, shouldn't you have told the police officer who just left? You knew him."

That, she thought, was a valid question. Narrowing her eyes, she switched her eyes back to her stepbrother. He sighed, then he grabbed the chair and motioned for his friend to sit. While Ben cautiously settled himself, his eyes wary, Kurt strode to the other side of the room and pulled a second chair to the side of the bed. Sadie had the uncomfortable feeling that she was about to be interrogated.

"Okay, look, Sadie, I know you don't remember me, but I need you trust me. Okay?"

She nodded. "I believe that you are who you say. I'm sorry. I just don't remember anything!"

He sighed. "I know. I know. Look, the truth of the matter is that I think you are in danger, but I have no proof." He rubbed the back of his neck. "It's possible that it might be my fault. I think you might be in trouble because of my job."

Startled, Sadie forced herself to sit up straighter. She noticed that Ben sat forward, his gaze sharpening as he stared at her brother. The intensity of his glance made her momentarily lose focus on the conversation. When her brother began to speak again, she mentally shook herself and returned her attention to Kurt.

"Explain, please. How is it your fault that I may be in danger?" She stressed the word *may*, as she was still hoping it was all a bad nightmare and she would soon wake up with her memories intact.

"I can't get used to you not knowing things."

He wasn't the only one. Irritation stirred that he would find her amnesia an inconvenience. How did he think she felt?

"Kurt," Ben interrupted him, his deep voice rich with reprimand.

"Yeah, yeah, I know. That sounded really selfish. Sorry. I don't mean to be insensitive." He shoved a hand through his dark hair. "I'm a reporter. Nothing big. Smaller stories, mainly section B. I've slowly been getting more important stuff, though. Recently my boss put me on a new story. I can't tell you much about it, confidentiality and all, but I think I might have found something serious. Unfortunately, it's nothing I can take to the police. I have no actual evidence. Right now, I just have suspicions."

"One of your suspicions is that someone knows you're looking?" Ben asked.

"Yeah."

Sadie glanced from one man to the other. "I still don't understand how that affects me."

Kurt sighed. "It affects you because I think someone is telling me that you'll get hurt if I don't stop digging." Frustration rang in his voice. "I'm so close to finding something, so close, and I'm going to have to stop."

"Are you sure you can't go to the cops? That Keith seemed to like you well enough. Maybe he'd be able to find the information you are seeking."

Kurt snorted. "The moment it's learned I went to the

police, any chance I have of uncovering the facts are gone. My boss will never trust me with another major project again."

It wasn't her fault. She knew it wasn't her fault. But she couldn't stop the trickle of doubt and guilt that wound its way through her. A new fear surfaced.

"Will they still come after me, do you think?"

He didn't answer her, which was an answer in itself.

"Kurt, you have to protect your sister." Ben shoved his chair back. The sound of the four legs scraping the floor made her cringe. Ben stood and paced away from the bed. "Your family must be a priority."

She appreciated him stepping in to speak up for her, virtual stranger that she was.

"I know I have to protect her," Kurt snapped. "I just don't know how to do that. Even if I stop digging, they're still there and will most likely come after me and probably her. I have to get more information so I can go to the police. Once they are involved, I'm sure we can find more protection."

Ben didn't let up. "And until then? How do you intend to make sure she is safe before then?" The Amish man slowed his pacing and took a deep breath. She could tell he was struggling to remain calm, although she had no idea why he was so invested in what happened to her. Was it just because he was friends with Kurt?

"You don't need to worry," Kurt said, lifting his chin and crossing his arms. "I'll figure something out."

Sadie's jaw dropped open. She couldn't hide her surprise. Maybe she felt this way because she couldn't remember her brother, but she was not impressed with him right now. Shouldn't he be more concerned about her? And about his own safety? Although, she had to admit, she had no idea what he had gotten himself into. That was a definite negative about having amnesia.

She flicked a glance toward Ben. He obviously wasn't any happier with Kurt than she was. Even through the beard she could tell that his jaw was clenched. His brows were lowered, and his dark eyes were flashing. "I stood beside my seven-year-old son and watched your sister's car slam into a tree. I will never forget the sound it made. When I got to the car, I thought she was dead. It was horrifying. There was gasoline on the ground. My neighbor and I pulled her from the car, wondering if the car would explode at any moment. I came here this afternoon because neither my son nor I could stop wondering if the woman we had tried to save would survive."

Silence followed his words.

She was touched by the care he had shown her.

"Your son, is he all right?"

Ben's glance settled on her. The kindness in those deep, sad eyes struck her. "Yes, Nathaniel is *gut*. He is very worried about you."

Kurt sat forward and placed his elbows on his knees. "I'm worried, too. Don't think I'm not. I just don't know what to do. I can't even think of many friends you could stay with. It would be one thing if you could remember, but you'd be so vulnerable without your memory. Unless…"

Suddenly he sat forward. Excitement lit up his face. "I know exactly what I can do and where you can go."

"Where?" Sadie shivered with apprehension. She might not remember Kurt, but at least she was certain of who he was. The idea of staying with someone she didn't know made her uneasy.

Her stepbrother gave her his wide cheerful grin. "It's perfect. No one would think to look for you there, and I could continue digging until I find what I need."

"Where?" she asked again, growing more tense by the second.

"You can stay with Ben. No one would look for you in Amish country."

Ben gaped at his friend, certain he had missed something. Kurt was desperate; he could comprehend the feeling, even empathize with it. In addition to that, he and Kurt had known each other for several years. Ben was a carpenter by trade, and they had met several years back when Kurt was writing a story on local businesses. He had included a section on businesses within the Amish community and had come out to interview Ben. They had formed a connection. When Lydia became ill the following year, Kurt had gone out of his way to assist and to be a support to his friend. He was the one and only *Englischer* that Ben considered more than a mere acquaintance. In fact, when Ben had decided to move away from the district where he and Lydia had both grown up, Kurt had helped him locate a new home.

Even so, the idea of the attractive young *Englisch*

woman staying in his home was ridiculous. A widower did not ask a single woman to stay with him unchaperoned. It just wasn't done. He knew it would not be appropriate, and the gossip that would surely sprout from such an event could be devastating. Not to mention the trouble he would get in with the bishop.

Nee. He wanted to help. Truly he did. But not this way.

He tried to convince himself that he was making the right decision, but he couldn't keep the worry about what would happen to her once she left the hospital out of his mind. And almost as important, what he'd tell Nathaniel. His son had been almost in tears when Ben left to come to the hospital, afraid that the woman was dead.

With a start, he realized he was actually considering taking this woman into his home. He needed to put a stop to this foolishness.

"I am a widower," he told his friend sternly. "I cannot have a single woman living in my home, even temporarily, without a chaperone. You know this. That's not our way."

"I'm sure I'll be fine," a soft voice said. He turned his head and looked straight into eyes the color of warm caramel. Eyes that intrigued him, although he couldn't say why. "Please, don't worry about me."

He would worry, though. He knew he would. He just couldn't think of anything else to do. As he gazed into those eyes, he was reminded of someone, but the memory skirted just outside of his reach. This woman was familiar, somehow, but he knew that he had never met her. He shrugged the feeling away.

Kurt shifted in his chair, dragging Ben's attention away from the lovely *Englisch* woman with a bandage on her temple. He knew he was doing the right thing, but his conscience wasn't easy about it.

"I don't want to get you in trouble with your church. You know I don't. But isn't there a relative who could stay with you for a short time? Someone who could provide you with the chaperone you need? It will be for a short time. A week. Maybe two."

Before he could reply, Sadie turned her attention to Kurt with a puzzled frown on her face. "Don't I have a job? How is it that I can get away with just vanishing?"

Ben blinked. That was a very good question.

"You work as a high school counselor. There's no way you could go back to your job in the condition you're in. I have already contacted them and told them you've been in an accident. Obviously, they know nothing about the amnesia yet, but once they know, they'll agree. You have some sick time saved up, although only about three weeks. If it takes longer than that, you'll have to take unpaid leave."

Ben let their conversation wash over him without really hearing it. Every instinct he had was screaming at him that if he left her in the hospital, Sadie would still be in danger. The image of her pale and lifeless-appearing body trapped in her vehicle filled his mind. *Englischers* could be a very reckless and violent people. He still remembered the father of a childhood friend being murdered years ago by an *Englischer*. The killer, a local teenager, was still in prison.

He shook his head. He couldn't hold the actions of

one man against all *Englischers*. Kurt, despite his lack of common sense at times, had proven himself to be a good and loyal friend. Ben knew that their family had suffered tragedies.

He couldn't get involved, though.

He opened his mouth to tell his friend how sorry he was that he couldn't help. Instead, he found himself saying, "Let me think about this and see if there's a way I can make it work."

Relief filled Kurt's eyes and a wide grin broke over his face. What had he done? He glanced again at Sadie. Unlike her brother, she was frowning. He could see the slight furrow in her brow.

"Ben, I appreciate your willingness to consider helping me out. I know that you are friends." She waved a hand between two men. "I don't mean any offense, but I don't know you. I don't even know Kurt, not at the moment, but he is my stepbrother. But we haven't met before today."

Kurt stepped closer to the bed. "I would never let you stay with anyone who wasn't trustworthy. Ben is as fine a man as they come. I promise."

The exasperated glance she threw at her brother had Ben biting the inside of his lips to keep from smiling. She may have been injured, but she had fierceness inside her. He was glad to see that.

"How do I know that I can trust your word?" she asked. Kurt looked a little hurt at that, but it was a fair question. She shook her head and then winced. "It's just that if I am in danger, and right now we can't really prove that I am, I hate the thought that I would somehow be bringing that danger into his home. He has a little boy he has to look after."

His heart warmed that she was thinking about his son. He needed to get back home. He had left Nathaniel with Caleb and Lovina. If he didn't go soon, he'd be getting home after it started to get dark. He hadn't gotten a driver since he hadn't planned on being gone that long.

"I need to head for home. I just came to assure myself and Nathaniel that you were well."

She was, for now.

Ben slapped his hat back on his head as he exited the building and strode briskly to where he had left his buggy. It had grown colder while he'd been inside. The chill bit at him. He ignored it. It would grow much colder. Dealing with harsh weather was just a part of his life. He had lived his entire life in this part of Ohio. He expected he'd probably die here, as well. Although, he was over an hour from where he'd grown up. He refused to allow guilt to take root. He'd moved out of the heart of Amish country in Homes County to get away from the memories of his dead wife. And to escape the expectations of his family.

Would Sadie's brother talk her into staying with him? he wondered as he pulled away from the town. He didn't know if Kurt's worries were founded or not. However, he had never known Kurt to be fanciful. Kurt might sometimes act without thinking, but he did seem to be very observant, which was probably why he had been entrusted with what appeared to be a dangerous assignment at his job.

Ben mulled over the facts as he knew them throughout the rest of the evening. He found himself distracted, thinking about the young woman he'd rescued that afternoon. With no memories, how would she know who to trust? Anyone could pose as a friend. Her brother wouldn't be able to be with her at all times. Just how serious was this story Kurt was following? If what Kurt said was true, and Ben had no reason to believe it wasn't, he was entangled too deeply to get out of it now.

It was very unsettling to not know what they were going to do. Part of him hoped that they would decide not to bring Sadie out to his home. Then he could just wash his hands of the whole situation.

He didn't know if he would be able to rest easy, not knowing if she was safe. Somehow, when he had pulled her out of that car, he had become invested in making sure she survived. It didn't make any sense, nor was it wise to become so deeply enmeshed in her life. He couldn't help himself, though. Seeing her unconscious, knowing she might not be safe, sat heavily on his mind even as he went to bed that evening.

Tomorrow, he thought, could bring more complications into his life than he wanted. Or than he was prepared for.

THREE

Where was Kurt?

Sadie glanced at the clock on the wall for what must have been the twentieth time. He had promised to be at the hospital to pick her up by ten in the morning. It was now almost noon. She didn't know if she should be annoyed or worried, although in her present condition she was leaning more toward worried. Was such extreme tardiness something she should have expected from Kurt? She had no way of knowing, but that wasn't the impression she had gotten from him the day before.

She could try calling him again. The cell phone that his friend Ben had brought in was still lying where he'd left it. She had found Kurt's name and picture in her contacts. So she really did know him, even though she still couldn't recall a thing about him. She'd given herself a headache the night before, trying to remember anything about her life. It was all still blank.

Five more minutes passed. This was getting ridiculous.

A nurse walked in the room. "Honey, is your ride coming for you? Do you need us to call someone?"

Great, now the hospital was trying to kick her out.
She pasted on what she hoped was a pleasant smile that
disguised just how frayed her nerves truly were. "I'm
sure he'll be here soon. I'll give him another call."

"That's a good idea. Let me know if you need any
help."

The nurse gave her a comforting smile and retreated
out of the room. Sadie snatched the phone from the
table and tapped the phone icon next to her brother's
name again.

This time, the call was picked up. She barely let him
answer before she was talking. "Kurt? Where are you?
They need this room for another patient. Are you coming to pick me up?"

"Ah, yes, Sadie. I'll be there soon."

The phone disconnected. She stared at the device in
her hand, frowning. The voice was a bit muffled, but
it hadn't sounded like Kurt's. There had been a lot of
commotion in the background, though, so maybe she
was wrong.

She stilled. In her mind, she replayed the commotion. Had someone been shouting *run*?

She glanced again at the phone, shivering as a chill
settled into her body that had nothing to do with the
cold. Whoever he was running from, they had Kurt. She
had no way to prove it. It could have been another friend
who had answered his phone, but she knew it was not.

What she did know was that someone was coming
for her.

Galvanized into action, she jumped off the bed and
grabbed her coat. Kurt had been very sweet the night

before, leaving during dinner to bring her a change of clothes. Nothing fancy, just a simple pair of blue jeans and a T-shirt and a pink-and-purple flannel shirt. When she saw the clothes, though, she thought they must have been favorites, judging by the amount of wear in the knees and elbows. Which showed how well he knew his sister. What if she never got the chance to get to know him?

Stop it! This kind of thinking would get her nowhere. She could go to the police. She considered that option; surely it made the most sense. Except Kurt had been so adamant that he couldn't that she hesitated. She had no way of knowing if she'd put him in more danger by alerting the police. She didn't want to do that.

Nor could she go home. The ambulance driver had brought in her purse. She had her driver's license, so she knew where she lived. She also had an idea that if she went there, someone would be waiting for her. Panic started to churn inside her. Then she remembered. The early morning nurse had brought her a newspaper. There was a write-up of the accident in it. She snatched the paper. It gave the address where the crash had taken place. Ben had said that it happened right in front of his house.

She would go there. He wasn't really expecting her, even though they'd tossed the idea around of her staying with him. Last night she had not wanted to impose on him, a stranger. This morning, he was the only one she felt she could trust.

She made her decision. Grabbing up the newspaper and her purse, she left the room. The nurse at the station was talking with a doctor as Sadie strode by. She averted her face. Neither of them called out to her but continued what appeared to be an intense discussion about another patient. She rode the elevator down to the lobby, feeling the walls closing around her the entire time. She tensed as the door slid open with a soft whoosh, but no one was on the other side.

Relieved, she pulled the hood of her coat up, both to protect herself from the chilly air and to shield her face. She walked past the reception desk and out into the cold.

Now what? There was no one meeting her, and she had no car.

A car with a taxi sign pulled up in front of the hospital, and an older woman got out. She paid the driver and started to head toward the hospital.

Sadie looked around. No other taxis were in sight. This might be her only chance. She quickened her step, trying to hurry without drawing attention to herself. *Please, don't leave.*

The driver saw her and he smiled. She could almost see him mentally adding on another customer. "You need a ride, miss?"

She nodded. "Can you take me here?" She pointed at the address listed in the paper.

"Absolutely! That's about a twenty minute drive. That all right?"

"Fine." She hurriedly climbed into the vehicle. The driver, a young man in his twenties, pulled away from the curb and slid smoothly into the light traffic. She glanced back at where she'd just left.

A man was jogging from the parking lot toward the hospital. Pulling her hood so it hid the right side of her face, she looked away. Something about the man struck her as familiar. Half a memory of an angry face formed, then it faded. She had seen him before. And he scared her.

She had been right to leave the hospital. Whoever had answered her brother's phone probably had him, and they were apparently coming to get her, too.

She bit down on the panic that was screaming to get out. Ben was the only one she could go to. Maybe he'd know what to do.

Her phone vibrated. Hands shaking, she looked at the text.

I got away. Hide. Don't text back. Danger. No police.

Kurt had gotten away. The very fact that he told her not to text back reassured her that it really was Kurt and not someone trying to get to her.

When the driver pulled up at the large two-story farmhouse, she distractedly paid him. There was something very solid and comforting about the look of the house. And, she realized, something familiar. Not specifically about this house, but about the feel of the place.

This was not her first visit to an Amish home, she decided. For a moment, she tried to grasp at the memory, but gave up as it continued to evade her.

A young boy watched her approach from the wrap-around porch. He looked about seven. Ben's son was seven. She thought back briefly, trying to recall his name.

"Are you Nathaniel?" she asked gently.

He nodded, his eyes wide.

"Could you ask your father if he has a moment to talk? My name is Sadie."

The boy whirled around and dashed into the house, calling for his father. Sadie climbed the steps. The sudden adrenaline rush she had experienced as she escaped the hospital had gone, leaving her exhausted. Her bones felt like they had turned into half-cooked spaghetti. She just wanted to slump down against the wall and take a nap.

Footsteps pounded toward the door. She straightened her spine, embarrassed at her weakened state.

The man from the hospital appeared, his dark eyes astonished as he held open the door for her. His gaze swept the driveway behind her. Searching for Kurt, she realized. He wouldn't have expected her to show up alone.

When those eyes returned to her, she responded to the question in their depths.

"I need your help."

Ben stared at the woman in shock. He hadn't really thought that she would show up here, much less on her own. The silence between them stretched tensely before he realized that her face under the bandage on her temple was pale and drawn. There was an air of sorrow that hovered around her.

He was being rude. "Sadie. Come in. My son and I were getting ready to eat lunch. Please join us."

He could see the dismay that crossed her face and hurried to make her feel at ease. "It's no imposition. I made plenty."

He led the way into the kitchen. The little boy who'd greeted her sat at the table, his eyes excited. "Is it her, *Dat*? Is it the lady from the car?"

Ben chuckled. His son had run into the house telling him that the lady from the accident was at the door. Ben hadn't mentioned the idea that she might come and stay with them. The more he had thought about the idea, the more ludicrous it had seemed. He was a widower living with a young boy. Having a young woman in the house at night was not appropriate, and he didn't know who he could have stay with them. It would have been different had they been near his own family, but he and Nathaniel had moved to this district three years ago after Lydia was gone. They had friends, but no real family close by. He had done that on purpose, to escape from the expectations that he remarry and give Nathaniel a mother.

He had never expected to have her show up on his doorstep alone.

That alerted him that something had gone wrong. His stomach tightened. Kurt had been working on a sensitive project. A potentially dangerous one. Despite Ben's desire to keep his distance from the pretty *Englisch* woman, he needed to discover what had happened to Kurt.

The small group settled down to eat. Ben and Nathaniel both bowed their heads to pray silently, the way they always did before meals. When he opened his eyes, he saw that Sadie was staring at her plate uncomfortably. It had never occurred to him that she might not be a praying person. Kurt was, he knew, so Ben had assumed that his sister was, as well. Or had she forgotten?

That was an unsettling thought, that one might forget *Gott*. Even during the darkest times of his life, he never doubted that *Gott* was there. Truthfully, he had often wondered how he would have survived without his faith. Shame filled him when he realized that just a few minutes ago he had looked at this woman who was obviously in need and had basically been trying to decide how to best get rid of her because her presence in his life was not convenient. That was not who he was. That was not what he wanted to teach Nathaniel.

Questions burned inside of him. Questions that would have to wait until his son was no longer in the room.

"Sadie," he began the moment they finished eating and Nathaniel had skipped off. "Where is your stepbrother? I know we had talked about you coming out here, but I had gotten the impression that you didn't want to do that. Am I mistaken?"

The eyes that rose to meet his were wide with anxiety. "He never came to pick me up this morning. When I called his phone, someone else answered it. I could hear my brother yelling in the background for me to run. I think whoever he was investigating had found him." She reached into her back pocket and pulled out her phone.

"What—"

"Hang on," she shushed him. "I want to show you this text I received. I believe it's from my brother."

He read the text. No wonder she was terrified. Instinctively, he tilted his head and listened tensely. When he heard the sound of his son practicing his spelling words, he relaxed.

"Have any of your memories returned?" Anything she remembered could possibly help them right now. She shook her head, destroying that hope.

They both started when someone pounded on the front door. No one he knew would pound the door that way. And, he thought to himself, he didn't know anyone who would use the front door. Most people came around to the side.

He moved quickly across the house. He could see a young blond man standing outside. The man wasn't looking into the house; instead, he was glancing wildly around him as if searching for someone. Even standing as he was, inside, Ben could see that the man was bouncing on the balls of his feet, almost as if he was ready to be off in an instant.

"That's the taxi driver who brought me here," Sadie whispered at Ben's back. "He wasn't as jittery when I saw him before. Something must've happened."

Ben waved her back, motioning for her to stay out of sight. She gave him a disgruntled look but complied. Only when he was sure that she was not visible from outside did he open the door. No doubt she was still listening. He schooled his face into a bland expression. At least, he hoped he did.

"May I help you?"

"Where is she? That lady I dropped off here a while ago? She still here?"

The questions shot out of the young man so fast that they blended into each other. Ben couldn't very well say that he didn't know who the man was talking about. The man had probably seen her talking to Nathaniel before he left. He hesitated to give any clue about Sadie's whereabouts, however. His instincts said that the driver was honestly concerned about her, but his instincts had been off before.

"Why do you want to know?"

The driver glanced around hurriedly again. "Look, I think she's in trouble."

So did Ben. If this young man had wanted to harm Sadie, he'd had plenty of opportunity when she was in his car. Making a decision, he motioned for the young man to enter the house. He shut the door and turned back to find that Sadie had stepped from her hiding place.

Upon seeing her, the young driver exclaimed in relief. "Man, I'm glad to see you!"

Ben saw her brow crease in consternation. She frowned and caught Ben's eye for a moment before she looked back at the driver.

"I'm sorry. I don't understand."

Visibly trying to collect himself, the driver shoved

both his hands through his hair. "I went back to the hospital. The woman I dropped off earlier had booked me to come back and pick her up at a certain time. When she got into the car, she was very excited. She was telling me all about how a man had come in searching for a young woman who had been in a car accident. He claimed to be a detective."

"He was no detective!" Sadie burst out.

Ben wanted to ask her how she knew that, considering she had no memory. He didn't, though, for the basic reason that he agreed with her. If Kurt was right, the man searching for her was not out to help her. He hated to think that anyone from the local police force could possibly be involved, but that would explain why Kurt was so hesitant to go to the police.

"I don't know who he was," the driver responded. "All I know is that my customer pointed out the man who was looking for you as we pulled away. He sure didn't look like any policeman I ever saw. He looked mean. When he reached into his jacket to get his phone out, I saw a gun. I don't know if you've ever had the feeling that someone was up to no good, but that was exactly the feeling I got."

Sadie had gone pale.

"Sadie, no one knows you're here."

"So will you help me?" Her voice was nearly steady, with the barest hint of a tremble. She'd leave if he said he didn't want the risk. He couldn't turn his back on her, though. It wasn't the way he'd been raised. One didn't ignore those in need just because it was inconvenient.

"*Jah*, I will help."

The smile that lit her face was dazzling, radiant with relief.

It shook him how much he liked being the cause of that smile.

"Look," the driver said, reaching into his back pocket and pulling out a card. His features weren't as strained as they had been moments ago when he arrived, but he still had an air of concern about him. "I think you're as safe here as anywhere. And the dude's probably right. I mean, I doubt anyone knows that you're here. But I want you to have my card, just in case you find that you don't feel safe. I would be happy to take you to the police, or if you think of somewhere else you think you should go. Just call me. Just tell me to pick you up at— what's your name?"

He directed this last toward Ben.

"Ben Mast." He was slightly amused at the earnestness in the young man's expression. And oddly touched. He was surprised to find an *Englisch* youth with such compassion.

The young man nodded. "Right. Tell me you're at Ben's. I'll know."

Sadie looked at the card, then back up at the young man. "Thank you, Braden. I appreciate your help today. I will hold on to this. If I need help, I'll call."

Braden took his leave. Within moments, Ben was left standing in his kitchen with his son and the woman who had literally crashed into their lives, and now threatened their peaceful existence with her mere presence in their home.

Gott, *please don't let me regret this decision.*

He wondered if the prayer was too late.

FOUR

Once the decision to allow Sadie to stay was made, there was no going back. But Ben could not allow an unmarried woman to remain in his house with only himself. Even if she remained hidden and no one else in the town was aware that there was an *Englisch* woman in his house, Nathaniel would know. Ben would not scandalize his young son by teaching him that it was okay to ignore the rules when they were not convenient.

And at the moment, the rules were the epitome of inconvenient. Still, rules were there for a reason. They helped to keep one out of temptation and close to *Gott*.

"You look very serious, Ben."

He hadn't realized that she had been observing him while he pondered the unique dilemma he found himself in.

He smiled at her, trying to ease the concern in her eyes. "*Jah*, I am trying to solve a problem."

"May I help?"

He could feel his smile wanting to change into a sarcastic smirk and kept his face still with effort. What would she say if he told her that she was the problem he was trying to solve? No doubt she would not be amused. *Nee*, he wouldn't be cruel. It was plain that she was feeling guilty about the situation she had put his family in. Not that he was blaming her. No one would choose to have someone chasing them. And she had to be going out of her mind worrying about her brother, the one solid connection she had at the moment.

"Listen, I need to go and talk with a neighbor. Could you stay here with Nathaniel for a few minutes? I will be back soon."

She nodded. "Of course. Whatever you need."

Ben passed her and headed out the door. Without thinking about it, he placed a comforting arm on her shoulder as he passed. He should have left without touching her. A jolt of electricity shocked him. She jumped, obviously having felt the same thing. Not *gut*.

Averting his gaze, he pretended that he hadn't felt the spark that shimmered between them, although he was fairly sure that his ears were turning red. Ben jammed his hat on his head and strode out, never looking back. He did not want to see the look on her face right now.

Jogging across the street to Caleb's house, he rapped sharply on the wooden door frame. Then he grimaced. It was not polite to pound on someone's door, but he was so rattled he was hardly thinking.

He could hear footsteps approaching, then the entrance was opened. Lovina looked surprised to see him.

"Ben? Is Nathaniel *gut*?"

"Jah." He nodded at the kind-hearted woman. Lovina was only a year or two older than his own twenty-six

years, but she seemed older. He could hear the chorus of young voices inside her house. She and Caleb had four *kinner*. She also had a widowed aunt living with her. "I was wondering if I might speak with you and Caleb. And Ruth."

Her eyes widened at the mention of her aunt. He didn't know Ruth that well, so it probably appeared to be a strange request. To his relief, she didn't argue or ask questions. "*Jah*, please come in."

He stepped inside as she left the room to gather her husband and her aunt. When the three returned, Ben cleared his throat. He had not planned what he would say, and the words seemed to stick in his throat. Finally, he drew in a deep breath and plunged into the story.

"Caleb, you remember that *Englisch* woman who crashed into the tree." It wasn't a question, for he didn't believe either of them would ever forget it. He would probably hear the sound of her car crunching against the tree in his nightmares.

"*Jah*, I remember well."

"Her name is Sadie. She is the sister of a friend I had met through my work. She has lost her memory, and her brother is not at home right now. I have been asked to look after her, at least, until he returns." He decided not to mention the true nature of Kurt's disappearance. "I told her I'd help, but—"

"Ack," Ruth broke in. "It is not proper for you to have a woman in your home without a chaperone."

Relieved that she understood the situation, Ben sighed. "*Jah*, but I believe I should help."

Ruth turned to her niece. "Lovina, I will be moving

in to the Mast *haus* for a few days." She raised an eyebrow at Ben. He felt like a schoolchild being scolded. "You have a place for me to sleep?"

"*Jah*, I have a spare room for you." He'd have slept in the barn, if necessary. Thankfully, that would not be needed.

"*Gut*. I will come over soon. You should not be in the *haus* alone with her."

"*Denke*, Ruth. I was in a bind."

The stern lines of her face softened. "*Gott* wants us to be charitable, Ben. He also wants us to guard ourselves."

He understood the warning and flushed.

Thanking his neighbors again, he left and rushed back to the house. The moment he entered, he saw that Sadie had cleaned up the lunch dishes and had started to sweep the kitchen. He appreciated it.

"*Denke* for cleaning up, Sadie." He glanced around the room. "Where did Nathaniel go?"

"He asked if he could go to his room for some quiet time. I told him that was fine. I figured you wouldn't want him to leave the house while you were gone. Not with all that's happened."

"You were right."

She narrowed her gaze slightly. "So? Have you solved your problem?"

He nodded. "I believe that I have."

She pulled the broom close to herself, holding on to it with both hands, and waited. She was a good listener, he decided, at least, when she wasn't feeling terrified.

"My neighbor's widowed aunt is coming to stay with

us," he announced. "That way, both our reputations are protected."

Her eyes widened. He could see the alarm in the stiffness of her posture. Raising his hands, he made a calming gesture. "I was vague in the details, but we can't stay here together like this. It wouldn't be proper."

Tilting her head, she frowned at him. "We weren't doing anything wrong."

"Maybe not," he acknowledged, "but it is the Plain way. Ruth will be here soon."

She opened her mouth, no doubt to ask another question, but the question was never voiced. Knuckles knocking against the screen door ended the conversation.

"Ben! I'm here!" Ruth's voice boomed through the door. Ben glanced at his companion, choking back a laugh at the amused expression on her face.

"Door's open, Ruth," he responded. The older woman entered the house, her sharp eyes zeroing in on the two people standing next to each other in the kitchen. It wasn't hard to read the reprimand in her stare. Ben found himself backing away from Sadie without even thinking about it. Then he flushed. They hadn't been standing that close, and Sadie was still holding onto the broom.

"You're Sadie, ain't so?" the older woman demanded, inspecting the *Englisch* woman.

"That's right." Sadie inspected her right back, the corner of her mouth lifting slightly. Apparently, she wasn't offended by Ruth's gruff ways.

"I'm sorry that you were in an accident," Ruth murmured, her eyes touching on the bandage adorning Sadie's temple. "Are you in any pain?"

"Not much. My head did ache yesterday, but today it feels a lot better."

Ben was relieved to know that her condition was improving. Ruth quickly got herself settled into one of the spare rooms on the second floor. He showed Sadie to the room across from that. Ben discreetly moved some of his own belongings from his bedroom to the bedroom on the first floor near the kitchen. It wouldn't do to have his room so close to their guest. Ruth gave him an approving nod as she observed his actions. It was all as it should be.

Nathaniel, of course, was thrilled to have so many people in their house. It was quite the adventure for him. Ruth was known for her skill at baking, and before they sat down for dinner the house was already filled with the aromas of cookies and a fresh pot of hearty stew. Sadie had pitched in and assisted her, and he noted that she was familiar with baking and cooking. It was interesting how the memory worked, that she could still manage to perform tasks that she had forgotten she had ever learned, but she couldn't recall basic information about herself.

The remainder of the day and evening went past in a blur. That night, as he lay in bed, Ben considered all the events of the day. Who was after her? Just as important as that question, what had happened to Kurt? Ben fell into a restless doze after eleven. The following morning he awoke to the crowing of the rooster, feeling as if he had not slept more than a few minutes. All he wanted to do was turn over and sleep for another hour.

With a sigh, he threw back his covers. Lack of rest was irrelevant. Chores still needed to be done. The animals needed to be fed and he had a job to do. Customers who depended on him. Crushing the wish to stay in bed longer, he rose and dressed quickly in the dark, then headed out to begin the day's work. By the time he returned from the barn, the rest of the household was awake, breakfast was on the table and strong black coffee was on the cookstove.

The next two days passed without incident. Sadie didn't say anything, but he knew that she never relaxed her guard. She peered out the window multiple times a day. He also noted that whenever she went outside, her eyes were constantly moving.

"Sadie," he said gently on the third day, "I will not let you come to harm." He immediately felt like a hypocrite. How could he promise such a thing? He hadn't even been aware enough to see that his Lydia had been terminally ill, yet here he was telling this strange woman that he would save her from an unknown danger.

Nee, not him. "*Gott* knows what the danger is. He can protect you."

She rolled her eyes but didn't respond for a moment. Then she sighed. "If only I knew that Kurt was okay."

He found her concern for her brother touching, and interesting, considering he was a virtual stranger to her. "Have you remembered anything, say?"

She shook her head with a grimace. "Not a thing. Although some things seem so familiar to me."

"*Jah?* Give me an example."

They were in his workshop. She moved over to stand near where he was sanding the top of a large square table. He made the mistake of looking up at her once. The way her brown hair was warmed by the sun streaming in the window made his heartbeat bump. Flushing, he forced his eyes back down to his work and kept them there.

"An example," she mused, reminding him of their conversation. "Well, for one thing, I love to bake with Ruth. And it's not like I'm learning. When we made dinner last night, I found myself handing her ingredients before she asked for them. I *knew* what the next steps were."

He frowned, recalling the meal the night before. It was a recipe that Ruth and Sadie had put together without any written instructions. It was also, he remembered, a traditional Amish recipe. Yet she had assisted as if she had been making it her whole life.

"I wonder where you learned to make the dumplings. It's not a recipe most *Englischers* would know."

"I have no idea."

Ben continued to consider the information long after she returned to the house. He imagined that Nathaniel had probably met her at the door. Several times in the past few days, he had stopped just to listen to the sound of Nathaniel's laughter. His son sure did enjoy having the attention of a woman. They both did. *Best not get too comfortable*, he warned himself. As soon as the danger was past, she'd be gone, back to where she belonged.

For she would return. There was nothing Nathaniel, or he, could do to change that fact. She was an *Englischer*, just like her brother. And as much as he liked and respected both of them, there was no place for a woman like her in his Amish world.

What was taking Nathaniel so long?

Sadie paced the length of the front room, keeping away from the large window, though her eyes continually strayed to it, straining to see outside.

Nathaniel had run upstairs to gather his spelling homework. He had come in after school yesterday waving his new words at her. His teacher gave them new vocabulary every Monday. This morning Sadie had promised that she would help him practice it after he finished his chores. The moment they were done, he had bounded up the stairs, yelling that he was ready to practice.

She grinned at the memory. She knew that she should not allow Nathaniel to worm his way into her heart. It wasn't fair to any of them. She was only there for a short time. Until Kurt was found and had enough evidence to go to the police.

And then she would leave.

She caught her breath at the ache the thought caused. Of leaving adorable Nathaniel, who held her heart in his small hand. Also, she realized, she was sad at the knowledge that she would be saying farewell to Ben, no doubt forever. The man could drive her nuts with his calm logic and his unflappable demeanor. Except she had caught him watching her a time or two. Could he sense the attraction between them? She smiled. Then she shook her head, hard.

She was a fool. Why on earth would she want any attraction, any sense of true emotion, to develop between her and the brave and faithful Amish father? A future between them was impossible.

She paced again, stopping at the bottom of the stairs.

Finally, Nathaniel ran down. His spelling words were not in his hands.

"I thought we were going to study," she chided gently.

The smile slid from her face as she took in the paleness of his face, the wideness of his brown eyes, as he stared up at her.

"Nathaniel! What's wrong? What happened?" She was vaguely aware that Ruth's singing in the kitchen paused. She didn't want the woman to know what was happening. She motioned for Nathaniel to join her on the other side of the room and indicated that he should keep his voice down.

Her heart thudded in her chest as fear spiked in her soul.

"I was looking out the window with these," he whispered, holding out a pair of binoculars. For the briefest second, she was distracted by the fact that he would use binoculars. "I saw a man with a gun. He looked mad. Sadie, I got scared."

The breath in her lungs seemed to grow heavy. Her head felt light. Could she have been found? She forced herself to be calm so that she would not make the child even more afraid than he was. Pressing her hand to her stomach to ease the twisting sensation inside, she focused on him.

"It's October. Maybe he was a hunter. Isn't it small game season right now?" She seemed to possess some basic knowledge of the sport and its timelines. She didn't think she was a hunter, but maybe Kurt was.

Nathaniel wasn't impressed. He gave her a look that would have amused her at any other time. At the moment, however, all she could think about was the cloud of danger she had brought to this peaceful household.

"Ain't no hunting rifle he was carrying. Hunters use rifles. This was one of those small guns, the size you might see an *Englisch* police officer carrying around. It didn't look like a police officer, though."

A chill settled over her. Somehow, she didn't think it was a cop, either.

"Nathaniel, what did he look like?"

"What did who look like?" Ben asked behind them. She had not heard him come home. Spinning, she came face-to-face with the man who was starting to take up way too much space in her thoughts. At his shoulder, Ruth was peeking into the room, her mouth pursed and her arms crossed. The option of keeping her out of what was really happened had just vanished.

"Dat!" Nathaniel dashed around Sadie and threw himself at his father's legs, the binoculars held tight in his fist. "I saw a bad man with my 'noculars. Maybe the man who wants to hurt Sadie."

The adults were silent. Sadie saw the same shock that was ricocheting through her stamped on Ben's face. They had thought they'd kept the truth from Nathaniel. Obviously he had been paying closer attention than they knew.

"A man is trying to hurt Sadie?" Ruth surged into the room, hands on her hips. "Ben Mast, what is your son talking about? I thought this girl was in an accident and lost her memory."

Oh, this had the potential to be bad. Sadie clenched her fists at her sides. Ben, fortunately, seemed to take the question in stride, although his jaw did tighten slightly.

"*Jah*, Sadie was in an accident, Ruth. Her memory is gone, hopefully only for a short time. All that is true. Also, her brother is a friend of mine who asked me if I could help out since he didn't want her to be home alone." His gaze flickered in Sadie's direction before returning to Ruth's stony countenance. "What I didn't tell you is that someone may or may not be trying to hurt her to get to her brother. We cannot confirm that."

"Ben." Sadie began to pace, unable to stand still, to keep the fear from becoming a solid mass in her gut. "I should never have come here. I will call Braden—"

"*Nee!*" The objection shot out of Ben so fast, so sharply, she stilled. Her eyes were wide as she turned to stare at her host. His jaw was set and his brow was lowered over fierce brown eyes that glared at her. "You are my guest. You are also the sister of a friend who asked for my assistance. The friend who stood by me when I buried my wife and Nathaniel's *mamm*."

She'd had no idea that he and Kurt were so close.

Ruth had opened her mouth, but at his words, her disapproving expression melted like chocolate left in the sun, and her eyes misted. "*Jah*, he sounds like a *wonderbar gut* friend, Ben."

Ben turned to the older woman. "One of the best friends a man could ask for. I would like to continue to assist him. He would never ask it of me if it was not important. And I cannot turn my back on someone in need, Ruth."

She nodded, understanding deep in her eyes.

Well, that was fine and good for them, but had they forgotten the little boy?

"Ben, I understand what you're saying, but Nathaniel."

His eyes met her, silencing her protest. The connection she had started to feel for this man bubbled up and filled the space between them. "*Jah*, Nathaniel needs to be protected, too."

He turned to face his son. Nathaniel stood straight, his young body tense. He should have still been afraid, but Sadie could detect the excitement vibrating off him. Now that his father was in the room, the boy no longer feared what was coming, but seemed to sense an adventure was about to commence. What was it about boys?

"How?" She voiced the question that had been bothering her. "How will we protect Nathaniel?"

He turned from her to watch out the window. "Nathaniel, can you describe the man you saw?"

He ignored her question. She held her silence for a moment, because she had learned that Ben was a deliberate man. He wasn't ignoring her to be rude. Chances were that Nathaniel's answers would be factored into his response.

Nathaniel shrugged, but his face was avid. "He was an *Englischer, Dat.*"

The sigh that left Ben made her want to smile, but she didn't. "I know that. What else did you notice? Hair color? Clothing?"

Nathaniel thought a moment. When he finally answered, Sadie paid close attention, the fist around her gut clenching tighter with each word. Blond hair cut close, angry face, a scar on his neck, she knew that Nathaniel had been right; the man was not a police officer. She knew because this was the same man she had seen at the hospital. And somewhere tucked in the memories she was trying so hard to access, she believed she would find more about him. He was so familiar.

"That's the man I saw the day I left the hospital. The man that answered Kurt's phone." She needed to tell them everything. "I don't remember the details, but I think I know him from somewhere. And everything in me tells me that he means me harm and will not hesitate to harm those around me."

Ben nodded, his face giving nothing away.

Ruth spoke up. "Plain folk don't get involved with the problems of the *Englisch* world, but you have given your word to help, Ben. I don't like this mess Sadie is in. *Gott* is strong." She nodded to herself. "*Gott* can help you with this."

Sadie appreciated the woman's confidence, but she wasn't sure that she agreed. Somehow she didn't feel like she was one who relied on God for much. She would never tell Ruth that, though she suspected that Ben had guessed her faith wasn't very strong.

"Sadie, I think it's time you contacted the police and told them that Kurt is missing."

"He didn't want them involved."

"*Jah*, but that was when he couldn't prove your life was in danger. I think it's clear now that both of you are in danger. If this is true, they may be able to find him."

It made sense. She left the others and went to her room to contact the police on her cell phone. When they insisted on coming to the farm to talk to her, she didn't feel she had a choice.

An hour later, a police cruiser arrived. A single officer emerged from the vehicle. His dark hair was nearly black. She guessed him to be in his late twenties. He knocked on the door. Ben answered, and although it had been his idea to contact the police, she could sense the reticence in his manner. She rolled her eyes.

"Ma'am." The officer greeted her. "I'm Sergeant Ryder Howard with the Waylan Grove Police Department. I was the officer you spoke with earlier. I went by your house. You live with your brother, correct?"

She hesitated. "I don't know what I can tell you, sergeant. I was in a car accident a few days ago and have lost my memory. Kurt asked me to come here because he and Ben are friends, and he believed his latest assignment may have put me at risk." Briefly she outlined having seen the man at the hospital and Nathaniel's seeing him in the area.

Concern shadowed the officer's eyes, even as his face remained neutral.

"Oh. Well, that's too bad. I can tell you that nothing looked out of place. There was no sign of forced entry.

No sign of upheaval. What was odd was that the front door was unlocked. When I contacted the paper, his editor said that Kurt was on assignment. He didn't feel there was anything odd about him being out of touch."

Sadie's shoulders slumped. Dejection welled up inside her. Was there nothing they could do?

"Miss Standings?"

"Yes, sergeant?"

"The fact that your brother was concerned and from what you have told me about the man you and the youngster have seen leads me to say, err on the side of caution. Come to the station, look through the profiles. If the man you saw is in them, it might help us. Either way, I would say you might want to find a different hiding place. We could probably locate one for you."

She blinked.

The police wanted her to go into hiding. She had hoped that her brother was being overprotective. But he hadn't been. Danger was, indeed, stalking her.

FIVE

Sadie sat beside Sergeant Howard in the cruiser, wishing that she had taken Ben up his offer to accompany her to the police station. He had done so much for her, though, and she knew that being in such a place would be uncomfortable for him. So she had told him that she would be fine.

As she had gotten into the car, he had watched her. She couldn't help but wonder if he was secretly glad to be rid of her, even if it was only for a few hours. She didn't think so. While he had accepted her decision, she sensed he was frustrated with it. Unhappy, even.

It made no sense, so she tucked it away and strove to focus on the task at hand.

Which was difficult, considering she couldn't help watching out for the man she'd seen at the hospital. A soft snort escaped her. Surely she didn't expect him to jump out at her, or to chase after a police car?

But she couldn't stop herself from scanning the roads around them and peering in the side mirror every minute or so to see if she could spot a man with close-cropped blond hair following them.

"We'll be there in under five," Sergeant Howard commented beside her. Apparently, she was transmitting her trepidation. For the fiftieth time since she'd entered the car, Sadie wished for the sturdy, reassuring presence of Ben beside her.

Stop it! It would be stupid to grow dependent on an Amish man.

She forced herself to put Ben out of her mind. When they pulled into the police station, she sucked in a deep breath and pasted a small smile on her face, attempting to project a calm and confidence that she definitely was not feeling.

Sergeant Howard led her into a room where he told her to take her time. For the next hour, she sat in front of a computer screen and poured over images.

And, suddenly, there he was. The man she had seen, his face angry and hard as his cold eyes stared out from the screen. She shivered. Deep in the recesses of her mind, she could hear a voice snarl. An image formed of this man standing over a body, a gun in his hand.

She squeezed her eyes tight to get the image to come into focus, but it was gone.

"This is the man," she said in a strangled rasp.

Sergeant Howard sat beside her. "Are you sure?"

She nodded. Now that she had seen the picture, she knew that she had seen him before. If only her memories would return.

"Mason Green. Hmm. He has a record for assault with a deadly weapon."

Sadie could well believe that. "I think he killed someone."

The police officer beside her sat up straight. "Why do you say that?"

It was too late to call back the words. The memory she had was so faint, she hesitated to tell him. But she knew she had to. Even if she was in error. "I could be wrong. My memory is weak, and I only get snatches at times. I have an image in my mind, and it looks as though he is standing over a body. I can't give you any more than that."

Still, he tried to pull more information from her until he was sure that she had given him all that she knew.

"It may not be a full memory, and it might not be accurate," he mused. "But I won't discount it, either. The fact that you may have seen him in your past and that he now seems to be following you is concerning."

She couldn't deny that. She was feeling a bit concerned herself.

The drive back to the Mast farm seemed to take much longer than the drive to the station. When they arrived, she drummed her fingers against the edge of the seat until the car was in Park. Then she was out of the car like a shot and up the stairs. By the time she arrived at the door, Ben was there holding it open for her.

His deep brown eyes searched her face, his frown growing fiercer, obviously not liking whatever he saw. "You found something."

"More than that. Ben, I think I remembered something."

At that statement, his brows rose.

She entered the house, aware of Ben and the officer behind her. Before beginning, she glanced cautiously around the room. This was not a conversation she wanted seven-year-old ears to hear. Ben seemed to understand.

"Ruth wanted to visit with Caleb and Lovina while you were gone. I sent Nathaniel with her. He was happy to get the opportunity to play with the other *kinner*."

It struck her suddenly that it may have been odd that she never needed an interpretation of any of the German terms that peppered the speech of her new Amish friends. Maybe she had other Amish friends she couldn't remember. Or maybe she worked with Amish people at one point in her life.

Not wanting to be distracted, she pushed the observation aside as unimportant and quickly related to Ben what she had learned at the station.

"This man has been in jail before?" he asked.

She was glad he was speaking. When she had finished telling him about the man she'd identified and her recovered partial memory, he had stood silent for a long moment, digesting the information. Too long. She had been close to asking if he was all right when he finally spoke.

She looked to Sergeant Howard for the answer to his question.

"Yes, Mason Green has been in and out of jail several times. Minor things, mostly. But the last time, he had assaulted someone and put them in the hospital. He was sent to jail but has been out for a year now. If he's out and about with a gun, though, he's in violation of his parole. That means he'll go in again when we catch him."

"If you catch him." Ben sighed and scraped his hands over his face.

Sadie ached at the trouble she was bringing to his door.

The officer didn't deny it, either, which was disturbing.

"Sadie." Ben broke into her thoughts. When she looked at him, his eyes appeared to be shuttered. She couldn't help but regret that he was withdrawing from her. Whatever connection there was between them, he plainly wished to break it.

"Yes?"

"This man you think he killed, are you sure you do not know who it is?"

Frustrated, she stalked away a few feet. "Don't you think I would tell you? Honestly, Ben, I've been racking my brains trying to figure it out. I just can't get a good sense of what's going on. It's driving me crazy, not being able to answer the simplest questions. And then there's all the things I seem to know but have no idea why I know them."

He nodded.

She waited. The seconds ticked by. Restless energy squirmed relentlessly up and down her arms and legs as she waited.

A loud whistle broke through the tension that had invaded the room. She jumped.

"Sorry. It's a call from my department." Sergeant Howard touched the radio attached to his shoulder and tilted his head, listening to the dispatcher's voice that exploded into the room in a static-infused burst.

"Gunshots have been reported..." The report continued. One person had been confirmed injured. The gunman had escaped. He was described as a white male, late twenties, one hundred and eighty pounds. Blond hair. A scar on his neck. As the dispatcher continued, Sadie felt her ears buzz, and she shook her head to stop the dizziness that attacked her. Mason Green had shot someone. She didn't know the area that well, but she was willing to guess that the shots fired had been close by.

As the message continued, she watched as the color leeched from Ben's face.

Sergeant Howard barked a question into the radio. When the dispatcher responded, he flipped the talk switch on the radio. "I'm a mile from the location. On my way."

He turned back to the two people watching him. "Green was apparently hiding in a barn, maybe to sleep, maybe for other purposes. When the property owner entered his barn and surprised him, it appears Green assaulted him. That's all I know at present."

"He didn't even know the man he shot." Ben's voice was flat. That did not bode well.

"I believe this was a case of the victim being in the wrong place at the wrong time. I don't need to tell you guys that he's dangerous. If you see him, do not approach. Call me. Sadie, you have the number to the police station. Use it. I have to go."

They both turned to watch him leave.

"Ben—" she began.

He didn't allow her to finish.

"That's less than a mile from here, Sadie." He stalked to the window and peered out, as if he would see Mason Green watching the house. "I need to go find my son. Then we need to decide our next move."

She watched him leave to retrieve Nathaniel, her heart breaking that she had brought disaster to their door. That even now, some stranger might be dead or dying because she had interrupted the peaceful existence of these people and forced herself upon them.

A sob burst from her mouth. She turned her gaze upward, appealing to the God that Ruth and Ben had such trust in. "God, why is this happening?"

She didn't expect an answer.

Hollowness swallowed her from the inside out. Mason Green was after her. He might have already killed Kurt. And it appeared he had no compunction about killing the innocent in his quest to find her.

Who would be next?

Ben didn't tell Lovina why Nathaniel needed to come home immediately.

"Ack, Ben. I'm sorry. Ruth needed to go visit her sister, who fell this morning. She should be back in the next thirty minutes or so."

When she fretted that Ruth wasn't home yet, he was actually relieved. He had some hard decisions to make.

"You can let her know that we don't need her to supervise anymore."

"Oh. *Gut.*" Lovina blinked at him, startled. He let

her think what she wanted. He needed to get his son home now and deal with the situation.

Nathaniel came when he was called. He started to pout at leaving his friends, but something in his father's eyes must have convinced that now was not a good time to test his parent's patience.

Ben bade Lovina goodbye, then headed for home, his stride long and impatient.

"Dat." Nathaniel tugged at his sleeve.

Beneath the youthful warble of his seven-year-old's voice, Ben grimaced when he detected the trace of fear. That man was prowling around his community, looking for Sadie. The fact that she couldn't remember why he would be after her didn't change the fact that her presence was what had lured him here. What if Mason Green wasn't alone? How many men were, in fact, after the pretty brunette?

He knew the man who had been shot. Listening to the dispatcher so calmly talk about someone he did business with being hurt, and possibly dying, caused a storm of emotions to fight for dominance in his soul. Hot anger began to kindle inside his gut. His son should be out playing with other boys his age. Instead, he was being put into danger by some strange *Englisch* woman just because her brother had a slight connection to him.

Immediately, shame washed over him. Had he forgotten every lesson his own *mamm* and *dat* had tried to instill in him? Not to mention the basic virtues of charity and hospitality. Not long ago, he had watched Sadie's car slam into a tree, and he had doubted she'd survive. Now he was begrudging her assistance when he knew her life was in danger.

Asking *Gott* for forgiveness, he entered the house and found Sadie pacing within. For some reason, the sight drove some of his anger away. It seemed that she was always pacing. Sadie Standings was not a very patient person.

"Dat?"

Shaking himself from the darkness of his thoughts, he smiled at Nathaniel. *"Jah*, Nathaniel?"

"I'm scared."

Sadie shifted, drawing Ben's attention back to her pale face. She caught his eyes.

"I shouldn't have come. I'm sorry, Ben. I wasn't thinking. I just got so anxious with Kurt not coming to get me and that man showing up. I never meant to put your family at risk." She tightened her jaw, visibly gathering up her courage. A spark of admiration for her flickered to life before he squashed it. "I still have my cell phone. I can call Braden. He left me his card, remember? I'm sure he would be willing to come and drive me somewhere else. Somewhere safe. Or maybe I can call Sergeant Howard back. He did say they sometimes put people in places to keep them safe."

Ben frowned. Where could she go to be safe? She had no memory. And what if the men had been able to track her because of the taxi driver? Right now, they hadn't found her. Yet. Although the men were close. Could Braden get here before these men found her? And as for going with the police, that might be her best option, but he didn't like the idea of leaving her with them. Even though he was the one who had insisted she go, now he wondered if it had made trouble for Kurt.

Was he even considering abandoning her and breaking his word?

Apparently, he was.

"Wait." He hadn't planned to speak, but the word popped out of his mouth. Sadie cast a guarded glance his way. He couldn't, wouldn't turn his back on someone in need. Lydia would have been ashamed of him if she had been alive here today. The thought of his wife sent another pain through his soul. Lydia wasn't here, though. If he had paid attention when she'd gotten sick, maybe they would have diagnosed her sooner and she would have been healed. She and their daughter might be alive today. But he hadn't, because his priorities had been skewed. He had been so busy with his work and other responsibilities, that he had failed to notice that his wife was ill.

Well, he was going to make sure his priorities were right this time, if only so that his son could see their faith in action. Squaring his shoulders, Ben took a single step toward Sadie. The movement had her turning her caramel-brown eyes his way. The sensation of familiarity that he'd experienced in the hospital struck him again. Briefly, it distracted him. He couldn't allow himself to be pulled away from his goal. He would get his son and Sadie to safety. But the moment he achieved that, she was no longer his responsibility.

"Sadie, your brother is a friend of mine. I will help you."

Hope stirred in her disturbing glance. Hopefully he wasn't making a mistake.

"Are you sure, Ben? You'll still help me?" she whispered, her voice soft, as if he'd change his mind if she spoke with her normal volume. Their eyes met, and he felt as if he were snared in a honey-brown net.

Nee, he wasn't sure at all. But he was too involved to back out now. "*Jah*, I will help. But we can't stay here."

"Where are we going, *Dat*?" Nathaniel piped up, interrupting the tension slowly building between the adults.

Ben pivoted to face his child and squatted to put himself closer to eye level with the boy. It would not be long before Nathaniel stood tall enough that Ben wouldn't need to do this.

"I think we should head out to see *Grossmamma* and *Grossdawdi*. That would be fun, *jah*?"

The boy's eyes widened. "True? Will I see my cousins?"

Ben's heart squeezed at the innocent question. The devastation of losing his wife and their unborn daughter had nearly killed him. He wasn't certain that it wouldn't have if he had not had Nathaniel to remind him daily that he had a reason to live. For that, he praised *Gott* every day. The community he'd grown up in, however, had ceased to be a refuge for him. Everywhere he went, the places and the people were only reminders of his loss. And when his parents began to pressure him to remarry, to give Nathaniel a new *mamm*, his very spirit had rebelled. He'd uprooted his son and moved to outside of Holmes County with a shocking rapidity. His family had been stunned.

It had never occurred to him that he was being

selfish, that his son may have needed more family than his father around him.

The emotion, the guilt, clogged his throat. "*Jah*, Nathaniel. I am sure that your cousins will be there. *Grossmamma* wrote and said that your *mamm's* cousin Isaac has returned to the Plain way. He has a new wife, he does."

Ben had always liked Isaac. They'd gotten into some mischief together as boys. It had saddened him when Isaac's brother died and Isaac abandoned the Plain life.

Ben grimaced. He hadn't abandoned the faith, but he had left his family when tragedy struck. He and Isaac were alike in more ways than he cared to admit.

"Won't your family object to your bringing a stranger, and a non-Amish woman, into their home?"

Standing, Ben turned to where Sadie was standing. He took a few steps toward her. The urge to put his hand on her shoulder and offer her comfort startled him, causing him to halt abruptly.

"My *mamm* would never turn anyone away, not when a body is in danger. *Nee*, they won't mind. They will be happy to have the opportunity to spend time with Nathaniel, too. It has been a while."

Nee, mamm would be happy enough to see them. *Dat* would, too, although Ben knew that his parents would both be concerned that he had nearly been alone with an *Englisch* woman.

"We'd best get moving. It's a long trip to my parents' home in a buggy. I don't know that I want to take the risk of calling the taxi driver. One less person who knows where we are, the safer we will be."

At least, that was what he was hoping.

In less than an hour they were tucked into the buggy. Ben sat up front, driving the horse. Sadie sat directly behind him with Nathaniel chattering away next to her. She answered his myriad questions with patience. Every time she spoke, Ben listened to her voice, the smooth-as-honey tones. He couldn't help himself. He was aware of her presence behind him to an alarming degree. Several times, he imagined that he could almost sense her eyes resting on him, even while she carried on a soft conversation with his son.

Flicking his wrists to snap the reins gently, Ben urged the horse to a trot once they reached the main road. The familiar rocking motion was soothing, even with the occasional jarring as the wheels hit a rock or a pothole. Relief filled him. He needed all his focus to be on the road, which meant he had to force his attention to stay off the woman he was helping. Traffic was heavier on the two-lane highway. The day was cool, with the scent of rain in the air. It would be hitting soon. Already the visibility was down. It was almost like riding inside of a cloud, the mist and fog were so heavy. His cheeks and beard grew damp as the first cold drops fell.

He sent a concerned glance at the sky. This was not ideal weather to travel in by buggy. If he'd had his druthers, he would have hired a driver. He wasn't worried for himself, although he could already tell that he was going to be chilled clean through before they stopped. Nathaniel, however, was still so young.

"Nathaniel." He heard Sadie's warm voice drifting

from the confines of the buggy. "Let's get you wrapped up under this blanket. We wouldn't want you to get sick."

Amazingly, the boy didn't argue at being treated like the child that he was.

Lightning sizzled ahead of them. Ben blinked at the brightness. That had been close. Thunder boomed three seconds later.

The storm was coming quick. He had no sooner thought it than the sky opened and the rain slashed down in sheets. Within seconds, he was drenched. Worse, he felt prickles of ice hit the bare skin on his face that was unprotected by the beard.

"I'm going to try and find a place we can wait out this storm," he yelled back to Sadie. "It's freezing rain. It won't be safe for us to continue on, especially not with the plows coming out."

Sadie leaned forward. He looked her way briefly. Her brows lowered, creating furrows in her otherwise smooth forehead. "Where?"

Ben's eyes swept the horizon. It was difficult to see far, but what he could see showed open highway.

Where was a very good question.

SIX

The longer he waited, the harder it became to see. As it was, it was like trying to see through a downpour of Ruth's famous split pea soup, the rain was so heavy. Heavy black clouds hovered over them like an ominous warning.

Thankfully, Sadie had made sure that Nathaniel was kept warm and dry inside the buggy. Which was more than could be said of Ben, but he wasn't about to complain. *Nee*, instead, he would thank *Gott* for keeping his son safe. And for keeping Sadie alive and well.

He heard her soft laugh echoing inside the buggy. He could imagine her face and the glow in her eyes without turning around. He frowned, the faint image in his mind, just out of reach, teased him. What was it about her that was so familiar?

His reverie was broken by a sharp crack. The horse shied, neighing frantically. Ben pulled gently on the reins, attempting to soothe the nervous beast. He scanned the area for a fallen branch or a limb hanging from a tree—something capable of making the loud sound. Nothing appeared out of the ordinary.

The loud crack happened again. This time, the horse reared up, nearly unseating Ben. A covey of birds in a nearby tree took flight, squawking and flapping madly. Ben didn't bother looking around to see where the sound had come from this time. This time, he recognized that sound. It was a gunshot.

The question was, where was the shooter?

Another shot rang out. Ben yelled as agony seared across his arm. All thought of searching for a safe refuge for the night vanished. His most pressing need was just to survive and to protect the two people in the buggy who were calling out an alarm.

"Hold on!" he shouted to them. "We are being shot at. I can't see a car. He must be on foot."

Gripping the reins firmly in his hands, Ben flicked his wrists, giving the command for the horse to gallop. It wasn't a command one usually made in weather like this. It wasn't safe to travel in a buggy at this high velocity. But he didn't have any choice. Somewhere nearby a man with a gun was using them for target practice. He didn't intend to stand still and let them be caught.

The frightened mare bolted forward, dragging the buggy with her. As her head turned slightly to the right, Ben had a brief glance of the wildness and fear within the mare's eye. He hoped he'd be able to stop her once they were safe from gunfire. He would not allow himself to imagine that they would not get out of danger.

Nathaniel screamed once behind him, then his voice dwindled to a whimper. Ben winced as his son's quiet sobs reached his ears. Nathaniel was not a crier. It tore him to pieces to hear Nathaniel weeping now. Unfortunately, there was nothing Ben could do about it.

Vaguely he was aware of Sadie trying to keep the child calm.

All of Ben's attention had to be on the horse and the road in front of them. The mare was zigzagging on the road at a full gallop. Once or twice the buggy tilted alarmingly. Ben gripped the reins tighter. The edge of the leather strap dug into his palm.

A new sound caught his attention. A low rumble, which quickly built to a harsh roar. Glancing behind, he saw a motorcycle coming up fast on their left side. The rider was hunkered down on the seat, his blond hair plastered to his head by the rain streaming down the side of his face.

Mason Green.

The fact that Green was on a motorcycle gave Ben and those he was trying to protect one advantage. Mason needed both hands to steer, which meant he had the gun tucked away somewhere. Hopefully, the man wouldn't figure out how to shoot and drive at the same time. They would be in real trouble then.

He must not have been a hunter, Ben thought fleetingly. If he had been, he wouldn't have had so much trouble hitting his target. Shaking his head to clear the rain from his eyes, he strained to see where he might possibly go to try and lose the motorcycle bearing down on them.

A horn honked in the distance ahead. A large delivery van was heading their way. Ben felt a spark of hope.

The road was too narrow to accommodate all of them. The motorcycle would have to back off. There was no way the biker could come up beside them with the van blocking the other lane. There was no shoulder on the right side of the road, so there was very little chance the bike would be able to approach them from that side, either. As the van got closer, the horse skirted to the edge of the road. One wheel of the buggy slipped over the edge and Ben could feel it sway. Ben leaned to the left, trying to balance it. It was no use. With a shudder, the vehicle hitched. Behind him, Sadie gasped and Nathaniel was sobbing. A splintering noise on his right told him some of the spokes on the wheel snapped. The buggy heaved to the side, throwing Ben clear.

He hit the ground with a thud, mud splattering his face and drenching his clothes. All of this was minor compared to the agony that shot up his arm as he landed on the gunshot wound. Ignoring the pain, he jumped to his feet.

"Dat! Dat!"

Ben turned and his eyes met the horror-stricken gaze of Sadie. She was struggling to escape from the wrecked vehicle. To his relief, both she and his son appeared to be uninjured, although Nathaniel was crying.

He couldn't let Sadie get out of the buggy. They were stopped, and a killer was right behind them.

"Nee, stay there," he called out, his eyes searching the area desperately to see where the biker was. To his surprise, the man who had just tried to kill them was not coming any closer.

The delivery van was beside them. As soon as it

passed, they would be in trouble. He opened his mouth to tell Sadie they were going to try and run down the embankment and escape.

The van didn't pass them. Instead, it pulled to a stop beside them and the driver stepped down and ran over to them.

Mason Green made a U-turn in the middle of the road and roared off in the opposite direction. They were safe for the moment.

How had he known that they were in the buggy?

A chill settled in his heart as he realized that Mason must have located his house and seen them leave. There was no other explanation. He had tracked them like a dog tracking a coon. As soon as he had determined they were away from anyone who could rescue them, he'd attacked.

"Sir, are you hurt? Can I help you folks?"

"Yes!" Sadie cried out from the confines of the buggy. "Stay here, Nathaniel."

Ben turned to watch her scramble out, her blue denim jeans incongruous with the Amish vehicle. His mind was going foggy with the pain from the combination of his wound and the jar of the fall. Otherwise, he might have been tempted to laugh at the sight. She was so small and slender—she couldn't have been more than five foot three or four—it seemed impossible that she would be able to bear up under the weight of everything she'd been through the past few days. But she had. Her expression was fierce and determined, her lips pressed together in a straight line. She was not beaten down. His heart was glad.

She strode to where the driver was standing over Ben. "My friend was injured, obviously. He may need an ambulance."

"I will not go to the hospital." Ben was adamant. The hospital could do nothing for him. He glanced down at his arm. It was bleeding, but not badly. His jacket had protected it, for the most part. All he required was a bandage.

Sadie gasped. She was staring at his sleeve in horror. Before she could say anything, he swayed on his feet. The delivery van driver grabbed his good arm, lending his assistance.

"Denke."

"Sure. Listen, I don't want to tell y'all what to do, but it sure does appear you should listen to the lady here. I can call 911 or I can drive you myself."

Ben shook his head. *"Nee.* I don't need an ambulance."

"Ben—"

"How's Nathaniel?" He cut her off, distracting her. "Are you *gut*, son?"

"Jah, Dat. I'm fine. That man was scary!"

That he was.

The driver was obviously conflicted. "Look, I can't just leave you sitting here in the middle of the road. Your go-cart or whatever you call it—" he gestured at the busted buggy "—is out of commission. And you all won't fit on the back of the mare."

"It's a buggy," Sadie replied.

"We don't ride horses," Ben said at the same time. Both facts were ridiculous and irrelevant at the moment. "Sadie, if you have your phone, you can call Sergeant Howard."

She shook her head. "I have it, but it's not charged at the moment." That made sense. There was no electricity at his house. "Even if it was charged, we need to get you and Nathaniel out of the cold as soon as humanly possible."

She was right. He wasn't as concerned about himself as he was about his son. And about her. She was a target out here. If the driver left, Mason Green might attack again. They had no way of knowing how far away he had gone.

"Could you give us a ride, maybe?" he asked the driver.

Relieved, the man nodded his head. "Absolutely. Where to? Want me to drive you home?"

Ben exchanged a glance with Sadie. They couldn't return to his house. Not now that they had proof that Mason Green had found Sadie and would kill her if he could.

"*Nee*. Not my *haus*. I'd appreciate it if you could drive us to the police station."

They received their share of odd looks as they traipsed into the station, that was for sure. To be fair, they probably didn't see very many bleeding Amish carpenters at the Waylan Grove police station. Nor did they normally see such men accompanied by young women in worn-out jeans and sneakers.

Sergeant Ryder Howard wasn't there when they arrived, but the chief of police, a lovely African-American woman with sharp eyes and short spikey hair in a stylish cut called him when Sadie introduced herself.

"He'll be here in fifteen minutes," the woman assured them. "I'm Chief Sheila Carson. We didn't get the opportunity to meet the other day when you were here. I have to let you know, your willingness to identify Mason Green might help us actually get him on charges that might lock him up for good."

"I hope so," Sadie said, her voice grim. She shuddered as she recalled the moment when Ben had toppled from the buggy. She'd thought for a moment that he'd been dead. "He came after us today and he shot my friend."

With an exclamation, Chief Carson turned to Ben, scouring him with a keen glance.

"Where were you hit?" she bit out.

"In the arm. I'm fine," he insisted.

"He refuses to go to the hospital," Sadie told the chief, frustrated at the stubbornness of the man. Didn't he realize that the injury could become infected? "If you have a first aid kit, I could look at my friend's arm while we wait for Sergeant Howard."

Within five minutes, Sadie and the Mast men were in the conference room, a first aid kit on the table. One of the officers had loaned her a charger, and her cell phone was plugged in. The chief had sent another one of the officers to the cafeteria to bring them something to eat while they waited. She wasn't that hungry, most likely due to nerves. But neither Ben nor his son seemed to have any trouble eating. Both of them had lowered their heads to pray silently, then they had silently scarfed down grilled cheese sandwiches, dipping them in bowls of steaming tomato soup. Nathaniel had wrinkled his nose at the first bite, and she had held in her laugh with difficulty. Ben had smirked, even as he took another mouthful.

"He's used to eating soup that was homemade," he explained. Ah. No doubt the soup was from a can, Sadie thought to herself.

"Okay, let me see your arm." She made her tone as no-nonsense as possible. He grumbled as he removed his coat, but she refused to give in. The least she could do was tend to his injury. He set his coat on a chair and rolled up his sleeve. Both items were torn where the bullet had hit.

The wound was just above the elbow. Had it been in a place where he'd have had to remove his shirt, she knew he never would have agreed to allow her to care for him. She could tell the situation made him uncomfortable, so she promised to hurry as she pulled on gloves and opened the kit.

When she saw where the bullet had grazed him, she sighed quietly. It was not nearly as bad as she had feared. Still, she was gentle as she cleaned the wound. It might have done better with a stitch or two, but she knew that wasn't going to happen. She applied a sterile dressing and taped it down.

"Keep this clean," she ordered him.

"*Jah*, I know what to do."

Did he really just roll his eyes at her?

With a small huff to disguise her grin, she gathered up the supplies, planning to remove her gloves and seal the bloody cloth inside them before discarding them. As her eyes moved to the blood on the white square of fabric, the room faded. Suddenly she heard voices as if from far away. A woman crying, loud harsh sobs, as if her world had shattered and she was left devastated. A man lay on the floor at Sadie's feet. It was the same man she had seen before, when she'd had a flashback of Mason Green. Now, though, she could clearly see the man. He was definitely dead, a gunshot wound gaping in his chest. His eyes, light brown in color, were open and staring.

He was Amish. She saw the hat lying beside him on the ground. The beard of a married man. No mustache. And again the woman crying.

"Sadie? Sadie!"

With a start, she came back to the present. Ben was standing in front of her, a concerned frown on his face. His left hand was raised, almost as if he wanted to touch her, to offer comfort, but wasn't sure if it was appropriate or if she'd accept comfort from him.

Nathaniel looked a little upset. She sent him a wobbly smile, desperate to hold the storm of emotions tamped down. For several seconds she battled. Then she made a mistake and looked back at Ben. He appeared to decide to risk her wrath and settled a warm hand on her shoulder.

"I'm here, Sadie. Did you remember something?"

It was more than she could take.

The tears she had dammed up burst forth in a torrent that shook her entire body. She couldn't breathe, she was sobbing so hard. She tried to stem the emotions, to get herself back under control. She placed both hands over her face, as if she could hide from him. She completely lost the battle when strong arms came around her, holding her close. Ben placed one hand on the back of her head and gently guided her face to his shoulder. She wept, and he accepted her tears, her pain, without a word.

"Am I interrupting something?"

Mortified, Sadie broke free of Ben's embrace. The shock of hearing Sergeant Howard's startled voice had the effect of drying up her tears instantly. Turning away, she rubbed her sleeve across her face, trying to scrub off the wet tracks on her cheeks. Not that he didn't already know she was upset.

A small hand crept into hers. Nathaniel. That sweet child. Without thinking, she stooped and kissed his forehead, letting him know she was fine.

"*Nee*, you're not interrupting." Ben responded to the officer's question, sounding remarkably calm and unperturbed. How she envied that! "I believe Sadie has remembered something. *Jah*, Sadie?"

Sergeant Howard's blue eyes flashed to her, alert. "Is that true? You've remembered something? Is it connected to what you remembered before?"

She didn't want to discuss it. However, knowing it might be important, she nodded reluctantly. "I'm pretty sure it is, yeah."

Biting her lip, she reached for the water she'd earlier ignored, more to give herself time to think than because she actually wanted it. The moment she took a swallow, though, she realized how dry her mouth and throat were. She gulped down half of the cold water.

When she set the glass down, Ben was still watching her, a slight smile tugging at his lips. She had chugged that pretty fast.

"Are you ready to tell us?"

"Sorry," she said, grimacing at the question. "I didn't realize how thirsty I was. I will tell you, but…" She cast a significant glance at Nathaniel.

"Ah, yes. One moment." The sergeant stepped out the door for a moment.

"Sadie, are you well?"

"Yes, I'm fine, Ben. If it will help them catch this guy, I will gladly tell them."

Sergeant Howard returned with a female in uniform and approached Nathaniel. "Hey, buddy, I want you to go with Officer Jill for a moment."

The woman held out a hand and smiled. Nathaniel gave his father a wild gaze but settled when his dad smiled calmly and told him to go.

The moment the two left, all attention returned to Sadie. She cleared her throat.

"Okay, then. Anyway, I don't know if your chief had mentioned it to you, but Mason Green chased us today and he shot Ben." She gestured toward the Amish man. Sergeant Howard nodded. Yes, he knew. That made it a bit easier. "So I asked her if I could clean the wound. When I was finished, I was picking up the cloths with his blood on it, you know? But suddenly, I wasn't here. I had a memory of a woman crying, and I saw a man lying on the ground, dead."

As she tended to do when she grew anxious, she paced a couple of steps away before turning back to them. "I'm sure it was the same man I saw before, only this time I saw his face. I didn't see Mason Green, but I saw the man he'd been standing over."

Feeling as if she had run out of air, she sucked in a deep breath before she finished describing the rest of the flashback, which was what she was positive it was. "The dead man? I don't know who he was, but he was an Amish man." She saw Ben straighten out of the corner of her eye, but kept her glance on the police officer.

"Amish?" He flicked a quick glance at Ben. "Are you sure?"

"Yeah. He had the beard, no mustache and a hat like Ben's. He also had brown eyes." This was part that really sounded crazy. "I think he had my eyes."

SEVEN

"What do you mean, he had your eyes?" The question erupted from Ben. When she winced, he realized he'd practically shouted at her. "Sorry. I didn't mean to yell. I am surprised."

Actually, he was shocked to his core. The implications of this memory, if it were true and if he were correct, could be devastating.

"I don't know, Ben. I really don't. I might be wrong. I probably am. But what if I'm not?"

Indeed.

He wished he could ask Kurt. Kurt had mentioned his sister many times. He adored his little sister. But never once had he hinted that the woman he considered his sibling might have Amish relatives somewhere. So where did that leave them?

"Hold on, Sadie. Are you saying you're Amish?" Sergeant Howard tilted his head and considered her.

"I have no idea. All I know is that my mother and Kurt's father got married sixteen years ago. My step-brother is missing. And Mason Green, the man who I think I might have remembered standing over the body of an Amish man I may be related to has shot my friend, and would probably have killed me and Ben and Nathaniel if he'd not been scared away by the delivery van driver."

Silence filled the conference room after her words.

"You have to go into hiding until this is over."

The sergeant's words dropped like pebbles into the tense silence. Ben watched her face pale. Just twenty minutes earlier, she'd been sobbing in his arms, her heart breaking. He couldn't bear to see her hurting. An urge to protect her rushed upon him. If the police moved her, what if she was still in danger?

"Let me take her to my community, where I grew up." The words fell from his lips before he'd thought them through. "That's where we were headed when he attacked us."

"I would think that he would find you."

"How?" Ben challenged. "He has no idea where I grew up. It's several hours from here, in a different district. And Plain folk are not likely to spill another's secrets to an *Englischer*. Not that many know my family. I moved here three years ago, and Nathaniel and I have mostly kept to ourselves. I think Mason Green followed a taxi driver who drove Sadie to my house to the area. If we travel in another vehicle, the chances of him finding us again are slim."

The man did not look convinced. A knock on the door halted the conversation. Jill, the officer who had taken Nathaniel, opened the door and let the little boy back into the room. Nathaniel went over to sit by a window, clearly worn out.

"Hey, Ryder. Sorry to disturb you. We have a call. All available personnel."

"We do? I didn't hear a call come through." Sergeant Howard thumbed his radio. Nothing happened. "Huh. My radio appears to be broken. Okay, look, Ben, Sadie. You guys wait here. We will figure this out, but first I need to go and see if I'm needed on this call. Don't go anywhere."

He followed Jill out the door. When the door shut, they listened to his hard shoes clomp away.

"I can't stay here."

Ben glanced to see that Sadie had moved to his side. His nose caught a faint whiff of her clean scent before he put a couple of inches between them. Unable to help himself, he put a hand on her arm.

"You want to leave?"

She searched his face, her gaze pleading. "I have to, Ben. I think that my memories are starting to come back to me. And I am desperate to keep trying to find Kurt. If they hide me away somewhere, my hands are tied. Plus, I'd be alone. Alone and helpless, with no way to find the truth. I don't like that."

He wouldn't, either.

"*Gut.* We will wait until the police have left, then we will keep moving toward where my family is."

Astonishment lit her face. "You still want to go with me? What if I bring danger to your family?"

"Sadie, I was honest when I said I think my old district is the safest place for you. We must trust in *Gott*. He will protect us."

She breathed out a half laugh, half sigh. "I don't even know if I am a person of faith. It feels strange, though, hearing people talking about trusting God. I mean, how can you when so much bad happens?"

"*Jah*, I felt that way when my wife died," he murmured, keeping his voice pitched low so that Nathaniel wouldn't hear him. "For a time, I thought *Gott* had abandoned us. Abandoned me when He took my beautiful bride and my baby girl."

"How did you ever trust Him again?"

"I don't know how I would have gotten through that dark time without *Gott* in my life. He helped me see that bad things are not His plan, but that He does have a plan. I trust Him to know what is best for me."

She didn't look convinced. Given what had happened to her in the recent past, he couldn't say that he blamed her. How did you explain trusting *Gott* when your life was in chaos?

"If we are going to go, we need to go now." He picked up his coat and put it on again, careful not to irritate his wound. "Nathaniel, *cumme*. We must go."

"Goin' to *Grossmamma's haus, Dat*?"

He felt a twinge of guilt at the boy's tired voice. "*Jah*. We are going to *Grossmamma's haus*."

"How will we travel?" Sadie murmured, donning her own coat. She walked over to the far wall and unplugged her phone. "It's fully charged."

That gave him an idea.

"Do you still have Braden's number? Maybe he can recommend a driver we can trust."

In reply, she pushed a button on her phone and it sprang to life. "I saved his number in my contacts."

He waited while she called the driver. Impatience danced up and down his spine. He held himself still with an effort, refusing to fidget as if he were a *kind*.

"Hey Braden, it's me. Sadie. Listen we need a ride… Well, we're worried that the man after me might know your car, he came after me." Ben could hear the exclamation coming through the phone. He smiled briefly. "Oh, really? That sounds great. Thanks. Here."

To his surprise, she handed him the phone. "He said his own car broke down and is in the shop. He has a rental now that he normally wouldn't be caught in. He'll give us a ride in that without charge. No one should recognize it, but I don't know where to tell him to meet us."

Ben took the phone gingerly, more uncomfortable than he'd been in a long time, but this was an emergency. His bishop did allow them to use cell phones if it was really necessary. In the fewest words possible, he gave the driver directions to an intersection several blocks away. He didn't want the police seeing them getting into a car in front of the station. Or anyone else.

He handed the phone back to Sadie. "*Cumme.* We must go."

It was a true testament to how serious his tone was that the exhausted Nathaniel didn't even make a token protest as they left the station and walked the several blocks to meet up with Braden, even though it was still raining. They didn't recognize the car, of course. It was only when he pulled directly in front of them and rolled the window down that they knew him.

The moment they heard his doors unlock, the three runaways jumped in, scurrying across the back seat, Nathaniel in the middle. Braden put the car in Drive and started forward. Ben laid his head against the back of the seat for a second, allowing some of the tension that had gripped him to flow out.

"Where to, man?" Braden looked at them through the rearview mirror.

Ben gave him the address and the young man plugged it into his GPS.

As the miles ticked away, he couldn't quite shake the worry that Mason Green was still out there. Nor could he forget the flashbacks that Sadie was experiencing.

What if the amnesia she was afflicted with hid a dark secret? One that could hurt her as much as Mason Green?

How was he to protect her and his family from a danger that she couldn't remember?

The windshield wipers were set on high, swishing back and forth at full speed to keep up with the onslaught of rain streaming down the windshield. It was coming down so hard now that it wasn't even possible to distinguish drops. Rather, it was a constant sheet of water. When they had first gotten on the interstate highway, the traffic was flowing nicely at around sixty miles an hour. They certainly weren't going sixty now. She leaned forward so that she could peer over and see the speedometer. Just over forty. Great. Well, the one positive was that nearly everyone else had slowed down, too.

Sighing, she settled back against the seat. Ben reached across Nathaniel and tapped her shoulder to get her attention. "Relax. We're on our way to a new place in a car the man after you has not seen before."

He removed his arm and she immediately felt the loss. Which was just silly. She did not need to develop a crush on a man so out of her reach. Even if he was kind and brave.

And thoughts about him would not be a good idea either. She tossed him a smile to let him know she had heard him, then turned her head to watch the rain sliding down the window.

Nathaniel slumped against her right arm, his even breathing deepening to soft little snorting snores. It was adorable. She smiled down at the child snuggled up to her so trustingly. Ben shifted in his seat near the window. When she lifted her gaze, her heart melted at the tender expression on his face as he watched his son sleep. A rather robust snore escaped from Nathaniel. All three of the adults in the car chuckled softly. She was still laughing when her gaze rose and snared Ben's.

All laughter fled. The electricity that had been simmering between them for days flared to life. He had the deepest eyes she had ever seen. The rain pounding on the car, the radio quietly playing in the front of the vehicle, all of it faded until she was aware of nothing except the strong man sitting so close to her, with only a sleeping child separating them.

"Guys, we have a problem." Braden's voice was

like being doused with icy water. Both Ben and Sadie jumped, their faces flushing. The sudden movement woke up Nathaniel. The child sat up straight with a cry.

"*Dat!* What's happening?" The fear in his young voice shredded her heart to pieces. No child should have to be afraid. Without thinking about it, she looped her arm around his slender shoulders and hauled him closer to her.

"*Alles ist gut*, Nathaniel," she murmured, the words for *all is well* flowing off her tongue like smooth cream. The moment the words left her mouth, she stiffened, her eyes opening wide. How had she known that phrase? Was it something she'd heard from Ben or Ruth? And why had it felt so natural to say it? Even if she had heard it, it shouldn't have been her instinctive way to comfort him.

"Sadie—" Ben begin, his face covered in confusion.

The car slid slightly before Braden corrected it.

"What's the issue?" she asked the driver, keeping her tone calm. She shared a glance with Ben. That conversation would have to wait.

Now that she was paying attention, she realized that they had slowed down. A lot. The rain hitting the windshield had altered. She could hear some of the drops *plink* as they made contact with the glass. Plink was not a word that should be associated with rain.

"Is that ice?" Ben asked, leaning forward slightly.

"Sure is. The road is getting slippy." She might have found the local word for *slippery* quaint and amusing if the situation hadn't been so treacherous. Knots were beginning to form between her shoulders as the tension inside her ratcheted up a notch. "I might need to take the back roads. The traffic won't be as heavy there."

"If that's what you think is best," Ben responded. She could see the crease that formed on his brow. He might have sounded calm, but he was worried; she could see the concern hovering in the deep shadows of his eyes.

God, if You're there, please help us. Protect Ben and Nathaniel and let us get to his home.

The prayer sprang from the depths of her soul. She had no idea if she was normally a praying person or not, but right at this moment, she knew that no one but the Almighty could get them out of the current mess they were in.

A semi truck zoomed past them, its speed creating a vortex that sucked them toward the fast lane. Sadie tightened her grip on Nathaniel and squeezed her eyes shut. Then they shot open again when Ben's hand closed over hers. He pulled it back when she looked at him. She knew he had been silently offering her encouragement, but it felt like more.

"Idiot driver. Does he think it's summertime?" Braden muttered darkly.

Once the car was no longer being pulled to the side, he sighed. A few minutes later, he moved up behind a slower-moving car. He switched lanes, passing a large sedan inching along. Sadie looked over. The woman at the wheel was staring ahead, her hands clenched on the wheel in concentration. This weather was an accident waiting to happen.

No sooner had the thought crossed her mind, then Braden exclaimed, his foot hitting the brake. She could feel the shudder as the antilock brakes kicked on and the vehicle began to skid. Outside the car, the air screeched with the horrendous clatter of metal crunching against metal. The semi that had passed them so blithely earlier had jackknifed and was completely blocking the road. Several cars had collided in their attempt to avoid the rig. Drivers were climbing out of the vehicles. She couldn't hear them, but it was obvious by their agitated movements that some of them were shouting. Fists were shaken in the air.

The violence of it disturbed her.

Even more disturbing, though, was the knowledge that they were not going to be able to follow through with their plans of traveling to the next exit and getting off the interstate. Which meant they wouldn't be able to use the back roads to get the remainder of the distance to Ben's family's home.

They were stuck, here in the middle of nowhere, on an icy interstate filled with other irate travelers. And the weather appeared to be growing worse. The icy downpour had become more snow than rain in the past few minutes while they'd been sitting still.

What if Mason Green was in one of the vehicles that was halting behind them? Granted, he didn't know what car Braden was driving. But they lost the advantage while they were sitting in an unmoving vehicle. All he had to do was get out of his vehicle and walk along the center of the road between the two eastbound lanes to see if he could find them inside the car. If he found them here, how would they protect themselves?

He really wasn't after Ben, Nathaniel or Braden. She

knew that if he found them, she'd leave with Green to protect the others. Although she didn't think they would just let her go.

And that would put them in even more danger. She had no doubt Green would willingly shoot her companions to get to her.

The image of him standing over the body of another man intruded once again. Her stomach curdled. She swallowed hard and tried to breathe in through her nose to control the roiling of her gut. Fear prickled her skin, like tiny insects crawling over her.

"We can't just sit here!" she burst out.

"I'm really sorry," Braden said, lifting his hands in a helpless gesture. His face was frustrated. "There's nothing more I can do right now. Hopefully they'll be able to get some tow trucks and a crew out to move the semi and get us moving again. Until then, I'm going to have to sit right here. I don't like it, either."

"That doesn't mean we have to stay here," Ben said, his voice slow and considering. He was obviously working on an idea even as he spoke.

Sadie switched her eyes to the Amish man sitting so close to her. "What do you mean? What else can we do?"

He glanced quickly at his son before meeting her eyes. "We're not that far from my old District. It's cold out, but we're dressed warm. We could probably walk the rest of the distance."

She pondered his words, mentally balancing the pros and cons. It might be their best option. Still, she hesitated to agree.

"Would that be too much for—" She really didn't want to say Nathaniel's name out loud, knowing that any sign that she felt he was weak would infuriate the seven-year-old. But her concern was real. It would be a lot to ask of the child. It was wet and slippery out, and judging by the way the trees on the side of the road were swaying, the wind was fierce.

Ben frowned, his own gaze troubled. "*Nee*, I think not. It will be hard. I do not know what else to do."

Biting her lip, she thought about it. "Ben, you and Nathaniel could go. He won't be after you if I'm not with—"

"*Nee.*" He glared at her. "We all go, or we all stay. *Wir bleiben zusammen.*"

The last was said deliberately. Nathaniel nodded with his father. "*Jah.*"

Her breath shuddered out of her. Maybe she was wrong, but she was pretty sure she knew what he had said. *We stay together.*

His satisfied expression told her she was right. Why had she known that? Had she taken German in high school? Somehow, she doubted it. This felt more natural than a memory from a class years ago.

"Are you guys sure about this?" Braden asked.

"*Jah. Denke* for your help. We will walk from here."

The young man hit the door locks and his passengers all climbed out of the vehicle. They walked as quickly as they could over the slippery surface of the black top covered with a thin layer of black ice. Ben assisted them over the guard rail and the silent trio began to make the slow trek down the shallow embankment.

The trees seemed so far away. Until they made it, they would be out in the open. She was aware of Ben moving to walk behind them. Not because he was slower, she realized, but because he was sheltering them with his body. Anyone coming after them would have to get past him.

Their pace was slower than she would have liked but it couldn't be helped. They were walking in thick mud, which sucked her boots in and made them feel like they had lead weights in the bottoms. Then there was Nathaniel. He wasn't a complainer, which she truly appreciated, but he was only seven. His legs couldn't match the long strides she would have used without him.

She flicked an angst-ridden gaze back toward the interstate they'd abandoned. The cars were backed up for as far as they could see. Was Mason Green among them? She couldn't shake the feeling that they had targets on their backs. Anyone looking their way would see them.

After what felt like forever, they reached the tree line.

As they ducked behind the large pines and slipped into the shadows, she looked back one final time, feeling as if she were under a microscope. Had they been noticed?

Heart pounding, she plunged into the cover of the trees.

EIGHT

They hadn't gone far before Sadie became aware of an echo behind them. She paused, pulling Ben and Nathaniel to a stop again. She held her breath, hoping to be proven wrong. There it was… Footsteps. Then suddenly the noise stopped.

They were being followed.

Sadie and Ben looked around. When they glanced back at each other, they both shook their heads. They couldn't see anything. Ben pointed down. She nodded. She knew his thought matched her own. Whoever was following them was using their footprints as a guide.

Grabbing Nathaniel's hands, Ben whispered to his son to stay quiet and follow. He led them off the path. They went down, down, down an incline. The rocks were slippery and they had to watch their step, but there would be no prints. That was an advantage. Her left foot skidded a bit on the slick surface. Any advantage they had would be lost if she fell down the incline and made a racket that would draw the killer to their position.

Ben seemed to know where he was going, she noted

with relief. He'd grown up in this area, she reminded herself. It made sense that he would know his way around. He wore an air of confidence that gave her some hope that they could survive their current situation.

"*Cumme*, Nathaniel. Let me help you down."

Nathaniel sucked in his lower lip. The poor thing looked scared to death, but he obeyed his parent without question. Ben jumped down one particularly steep part, then reached up his arms for his son. Effortlessly, he swung the boy down by his side. Sadie was impressed with the unconscious show of his physical strength.

Her admiration changed to alarm when the man turned back to her. She gulped. There was not much she could do. She had to get down there, and they didn't have the luxury of time to let her try and make her own slow way down.

She allowed herself to lean into Ben's arms, setting her hands on his shoulders to keep her balance. When he pulled her down and swung her to his side, a strange breathlessness stole over her.

It may have been her imagination, but she thought that he held on to her a second or two longer than necessary. Then again, he might have been trying to ascertain if she was steady enough to stand on her own.

When he let go, she felt a pang of regret, but quickly shoved it aside. They didn't have time for her to be nonsensical.

Ben led his son and Sadie along a rocky path that wound through patches of mud-covered areas where the trees were less dense and erosion had worn away the rocks. They communicated mostly with gestures, as any sound could lead the villain hunting them down straight to them.

Suddenly, Ben stopped. Excitement filled him as he turned in a circle, looking around.

"Sadie," he whispered softly. "There's a cave near here. Its entrance is partially hidden by trees and shrubs. If we can get there, we can get out of the rain."

He cast a glance meaningfully behind them. She nodded to show she comprehended the secret message. If they hid in the cave, it might throw whoever was following them off the track long enough for them to escape.

"It's worth a shot," she whispered back.

"We're going to go to a cave?" Nathaniel didn't sound excited. She looked at Ben and could see the compassion there. Ben knew his son did not like the dark. A dark cave would not be his son's choice for an adventure.

"*Jah.* Sadie and I will be with you. Maybe we can dry off some, ain't so?"

The sigh that came out of the child lifted his shoulders in an exaggerated motion. Sadie saw Ben bite back a smile. The little boy was so endearing, Sadie covered her mouth with her hand so he wouldn't think she was laughing at him.

"Guess so, *Dat.*"

Her heart melted at the brave acceptance. Putting her arm around his shoulders, she gave Nathaniel a gentle squeeze. "I don't like caves, either, but your father is right that it would be good to get out of the rain."

She was afraid to say more. Even though they were whispering and couldn't hear any steps behind them, it didn't mean that they were out of danger. Or out of earshot.

Keeping a firm hand in Nathaniel's, she followed Ben until they came to the mouth of the cave. He was right. The entrance was partially hidden. She might have missed it altogether had he not been there with her.

Hopefully, the person following them, whether it was Mason Green or someone else, wasn't familiar with the surroundings. If he wasn't, they might be able to hide out and escape.

Unfortunately, inside a cave hewn out of stone on a cold October day wasn't a warm place to be. With their clothes damp from the weather, it wasn't long before teeth started chattering.

Shivering, she moved beside Nathaniel and pulled him into her arms, trying to warm the little boy. She was shocked when Ben stepped to his other side and pulled both of them into his arms. She knew it was just from necessity. There was nothing romantic in the embrace. It was purely for the sake of survival.

Telling herself that, however, did nothing to stop the red tide of hot color that she could feel flooding her neck and up into her face. Her heartbeat kicked up. She was amazed that neither Nathaniel nor Ben seemed to be aware of how affected she was by the group embrace.

A scratching outside the cave got their attention.

Trepidation stole over her. The muscles in her shoulders and neck bunched. Something—or someone—was outside the cave. Whoever it was didn't seem to be trying to enter. She told herself it was probably an animal of some sort scavenging for the winter.

She didn't believe it. Whatever was out there was larger than a squirrel.

The hair stood up on the back of her neck. For no animal would have made that noise. It was a footstep, made by human feet.

Ben gestured for them to stay down. He went to peek out.

A second later, he rushed back inside. Unceremoniously, he lifted his son into his arms.

"Move," he hissed urgently.

She moved. They ran deeper inside the cave.

"We can't get out without being shot," he explained as they hurried. "It's Green. It looks like he's trying to blow up something at the entrance."

Horror shot through her. "We'll be trapped here."

No sooner had the words left her mouth than an explosion rocked the cave, showering rocks and debris in every direction.

The cave entrance disappeared in a hail of rocks, stones and debris. The blast knocked all of them to the ground. The cave had been shadowy and dim before. Now it was pitch black. Fear rose up inside Ben. Neither Nathaniel nor Sadie was making any sound. Frantically he sat up.

"Sadie? Nathaniel? Please answer." He held his breath as he crawled over the floor, searching for the others.

His fingers came in contact with Sadie's. He gripped her hand, and the backs of his eyes grew hot when she grabbed onto him. Nathaniel called out his name weakly. As quickly as he could, he followed his son's voice until he found him. The child was terrified, but Ben couldn't feel any wounds on him. He needed to know for sure.

"Are you hurt?" Ben asked them.

"I'm fine, but I can't see anything. What about you guys?" Sadie responded.

"I'm not hurt. Nathaniel?"

The dust settled around them. Nathaniel coughed a couple of times. He didn't appear to be experiencing difficulty breathing, however, and Ben murmured a prayer of thanksgiving. A hand reached out in the dark and touched his arm. Sadie. When her arm suddenly gripped his arm, he lifted a hand to cover it, attempting to reassure her.

"Dat?"

His heart clenched at the quaver in Nathaniel's voice.

"Jah, I'm here. We're fine." He kept his voice low, just in case Mason was standing on the other side of the debris that was now blocking their exit.

"What do we do, Ben?"

He was astounded by the trust in her words. And humbled. She was still trusting him, even after he had led them into what might seem like an impossible situation. Sadie wouldn't know it, but he had been inside this cave many times in his life. He had explored every inch of it during his teen years.

Hopefully Mason Green wasn't familiar with the terrain and this particular cave.

"I have an idea," he assured her. "It would help if we had some light."

"Light!" she echoed in a voice of surprise. "That I can help you with."

He heard her fumbling with something in the dark. After a few seconds, there was a click, and a bright beam of white light cut through the darkness, startling him.

"What—"

"I have a flashlight app on my phone."

Ah. He never knew that cell phones came with flashlights.

"What's your plan?" Sadie asked.

"I know this cave. If I remember correctly, there should be another way out."

She sighed. "That's great news. How deep is this cave until we can get to the exit? Do you recall?"

He scratched his head and realized his hat was gone. His hair was coated with debris. "*Nee*, I don't remember. It's been many years since I was here." He hoped that the other exit hadn't become overgrown or caved in. "Shine your light at the ground for a moment, please."

The light shifted lower. Seeing his hat, he bent down and grabbed it. "Walk close together."

He wondered if he should mention the possibility of meeting up with a wild critter or two in the cave. Part of him didn't want to cause them any more worry. On the other hand, it was best to be prepared.

He mentioned the caution to Sadie.

"Yay," she returned sarcastically. "I'll probably have a scared bat get stuck in my hair."

"Do you think we'll see a bear?" Nathaniel couldn't quite contain his excitement at the thought.

"Ah, I don't suppose we'll run into a bear."

"I should hope not," Sadie muttered. He smiled. She was adorable when she grew disgruntled. He had no business noticing that. His smile dropped from his face. Ben was starting to have his suspicions about Sadie's origins. She had some Plain in her background, he was sure of it. Little things about her told him that she wasn't unfamiliar with their ways, at least, not completely. Regardless, she was not Amish.

He needed to remember that. There was no future between them, and he could not allow himself to forget that or become overly friendly and give her the wrong idea.

Deliberately, he turned away and kept walking. They went deeper and deeper into the cave. The air was still and damp. There was a musty odor.

"Ew. It smells gross in here," Nathaniel commented.

Sadie snickered at the observation. Ben chuckled. Reaching back, he patted his son's shoulder.

"*Jah*, it does smell gross."

"Do you think the bad man is waiting for us?"

With a sigh, Ben pondered how to answer. He didn't want to scare his son, but he would never lie to him, either.

"I hope he has gone away," he said. "If he hasn't, we'll keep hiding from him."

Even to his own ears, the response lacked substance.

"I've been thinking, Ben," Sadie said into the darkness. "I know you believe that God is with us, right?"

He nodded. "*Jah*. With my whole being I believe that."

"So, if He is with us, then it is His job to protect us."

He wasn't sure he agreed with that assessment. It seemed too standoffish.

"*Nee*, not His job. He is our Father. We are His children. Sometimes sin affects the world and bad things do happen. That is true. But *Gott* is always there, loving His children and trying to keep them close to Him."

The light glanced off the walls, throwing long shadows against the floor.

"There's a bend up ahead," Ben announced, the words echoing around them.

He led the way, listening to the reassuring scrape of their boots on the bottom of the cave. He might not be able to see behind him very well, but at least he knew that they were following closely.

"Ben, is that a light ahead of us?" Sadie said at his shoulder.

He frowned. There was a light, but it wasn't as bright as he would have expected it to be. His heart fell at the thought that the second exit might not be viable. Maybe it was just dim due to the weather.

As the small group drew closer to the light, his fears were realized. The second exit was still there. However, the rocks around the exit had caved in. While not completely covered, he could see that they would have to dig themselves out if they wanted to use it. At present, it looked large enough for Nathaniel to squeeze through. Definitely not two full-grown adults.

He set his jaw. *Gott* was with them. He had shown them a way out. They had to work a bit to use the exit, but it was doable. Cautiously, Ben stepped closer to the hole in the pile blocking their way. Peering out, he looked as far as he could in every direction.

No Mason Green.

He bowed his head and sent up a prayer of thanksgiving.

"Are you praying?" Sadie whispered.

"*Jah.* I am thanking *Gott* that we have reached another way out and that no one is waiting for us."

He knew she'd understand.

"Um, we're going to have to dig our way out." She didn't sound too enthusiastic.

"*Jah.* We will dig. But we will get out."

A moment of silence met his declaration.

"You're right," she said finally. "I'm a bit embarrassed by my glass-half-empty attitude. Forgive me."

"Es ist nichts," he responded, telling her it was nothing. He was curious to see what her response would be. Would she understand the German words? He suspected that she would.

"It's nothing?" she replied, confirming his suspicions by correctly translating the phrase. "It's not nothing, Ben. I don't like knowing how cynical I am. We thought we were trapped, and you were right. God has shown us a way out, like you believed. And here I am complaining because I might have to lift a few rocks."

He didn't like the self-recriminations.

"Sadie, you are human. You have also had a very rough few days. It is time to forgive yourself and move on. We need to move these rocks. It will be dark by the time we arrive at my parents' house."

It was too bad it wasn't summer. If it had been, then

it wouldn't have been as urgent. They could have rested a bit, knowing that they had a few more hours of daylight. As it was, he knew that the sky would be dark within a few hours.

It took them almost an hour to dig the hole open enough to allow them to exit, one at a time. Ben went first, figuring that if Mason Green was out there, he would shoot him first, giving the other two a warning. He didn't even think about using himself as bait to protect the others. Some things, like family, were worth dying for. He was nonetheless highly relieved when he stood outside the cave in the cold, wet afternoon, unscathed except for a few additional scratches.

Nathaniel came out next, followed by Sadie. The weary trio glanced at the cave for a moment. He saw a shudder rip through Sadie.

"We could have died there," she said when her haunted gaze met his. "We came so close to losing everything."

"We didn't."

She nodded and they continued on with their journey.

They kept silent for the most part. Every now and then, he and Sadie would exchange a glance. They had shared a harrowing experience and both were exhausted. They couldn't rest, though.

Mason Green might think he had killed them in the explosion. It would be best if he did.

How long did they have until he realized that they were still alive?

NINE

They trudged on until Sadie felt as though her legs would fall off if she had to take yet another step. Still they kept going. Nathaniel had reached the limit of what he could bear with patience and was letting them know it. He whined about being tired and said his feet were frozen. Then he complained about how his stomach hurt, he was so hungry.

Sadie completely understood. Her own stomach was hollow. It had gone past the point of rumbling. Now, she was so weary she wasn't sure which was harder, the hunger or the exhaustion filling her limbs with lead.

And the thirst. She was also pretty sure she was slightly dehydrated. Her mouth was so dry, when she tried talking it felt as though the edges of her mouth were coated with cotton.

"*Dat*, my legs hurt." The strength had leeched from Nathaniel's protests and complaints. Now his whining had changed into whimpers.

Ben halted. He crouched down in front of his son. The sunlight had faded and now they were moving in the twilight. His features were blurry, but Sadie could detect the gentle care in the eyes glinting up from his bone-weary face.

"Nathaniel, we are very close to *Grossmamma's* house. I know this journey is difficult. You have been very brave, and I am proud of you. I need you to be strong for just a short while more. *Grossmamma* and *Grossdawdi* will be happy to see you. Can you be strong for a short while longer?" He tapped the boy's chin.

Nathaniel's chin wobbled. He nodded. Probably too tired to speak, she thought, pity for him sneaking up on her. Ben tousled his hair and stood, grabbing the youngster's hand as they continued on. If only Nathaniel were smaller, Ben might have been able to carry him on his shoulders.

Sadie was embarrassed at the tears that swam in her eyes. Yes, his warmth and caring for his child were precious, but certainly she shouldn't be crying over them.

It must be the exhaustion. That and the fact that her feet were just about numb from the frozen ground. At least it had stopped raining. Or snowing. She thrust her ice-cold hands into her pockets.

"Sadie?" Ben's quiet voice broke through her thoughts. Had he been talking to her?

"Sorry? I was thinking. Did you say something?"

"*Jah.* I asked you if you were well. I was serious. My parents live close now. Normally, I could walk there from here in about ten minutes."

"It's probably going to take longer with how tired we are."

Still, ten minutes. Even twenty. She could do it,

right? She had to. Even if she wasn't well, they had no choice but to keep moving on. Telling him her woes wouldn't improve their predicament. If anything, it would make him feel bad. And what about poor Nathaniel? If she faltered, what sort of example would that set for him? No, she would keep her aches and her problems to herself.

"Don't worry about me, Ben. I'm sure that we can make it. Especially if we are so close."

He didn't respond for the space of a heartbeat.

"I do worry, though. I know we couldn't wait in the car. It would have definitely been too dangerous for us. And for Braden. However, you were injured recently. This has been a hard journey, even without that."

Warmth tingled in her heart at his words. She tried not to let them get to her, but it wasn't working. This man was breaking through her defenses, and he wasn't even trying. She needed a distraction. She recalled his injured arm. Had that just been this morning?

"How is your arm?" He didn't seem to be favoring it. But then, maybe he was deliberately ignoring the discomfort.

"Ach. It's fine. I barely notice it."

Men. She rolled her eyes. She was pretty sure he was understating the matter.

A few more minutes of silence fell.

"*Dat!* Is that *Grossmamma's haus*?" Nathaniel seemed to regain some of his energy. It was contagious. She straightened her stiff shoulders as hope zinged through her. Could they be nearly at their destination?

The exuberance was clouded briefly by the worry

that his family would not want her there. She was an outsider. Not to mention the fact that Nathaniel and Ben had been through horrific things because of her presence in their lives. She should brace herself for their reaction.

She was so tired, though, she'd probably cry and embarrass herself if they didn't want her around. She shook herself free of her misgivings as they walked up the driveway of a large white farmhouse.

An image of another white house filled her mind. It was also two stories, but didn't have the large porch that stretched across the entire front of the house like the one on Ben's parents' house. The one in her mind had a small porch, just big enough for two or three people to stand on. She could see the blueish-gray door on the side. And the smell of apple pie, freshly baked. Her mouth watered.

As the memory, for she was sure that was what it was, faded, she couldn't get rid of the sense of familiarity as they walked up the steps to the door.

She was still in the thrall of these emotions when the door opened and an older Amish woman peered out.

"Ben? Nathaniel!" The woman opened the door, confusion in her eyes, although there was a wide smile on her face as she let her son and his companions into the house. There were no electric lamps inside. Instead, the light in the room was made by natural gas-fueled lights that hung on the walls. She was surprised that Ben's parents used these; she had expected kerosene lanterns. "Ach! You didn't tell me you were coming to visit. Where is your buggy?" She peered around them. "Did you already put your horse away?"

Her brow creased. No wonder.

"*Nee, Mamm.* We walked from the interstate."

Her eyes widened. "Walked?"

"*Grossmamma.*" Nathaniel captured her attention. "I'm hungry."

Her eyes caught her son's. Sadie could see the questions burning there, but the woman smiled at her grandson and bade him to go into the kitchen. She'd get him some food.

"*Mamm,*" Ben said as Nathaniel ran to the kitchen. "I will tell you everything, but first I want to introduce you to—"

Ben's mother turned expectantly to face her. As she took in Sadie's face, her mouth dropped open to form a round O.

"Hannah? Hannah Bontrager?"

Ben felt a shock go through him at the long-forgotten name. Hannah Bontrager had disappeared years ago. And so had her young daughter and his childhood friend, Sadie Ann. Was it possible? Could the woman he'd been assisting really be his friend who had disappeared years before?

Sadie shook her head, eyes wide with confusion. He thought he could also detect a speck of fear in her gaze.

"No, Mrs. Mast. My name's Sadie, not Hannah. Sadie Standings. My mother's name was Hannah, though."

His mother blinked, her eyes still dazed. She couldn't seem to stop looking at the *Englisch* woman standing in her home. Her eyes met his questioning. He shrugged and shook his head, confident that his mother would remember that Hannah had a daughter named Sadie. She nodded at him slightly, then returned her gaze to Sadie.

"Ack. Sorry. Of course, you could not be Hannah. She would be my age, not a young woman such as you. Come in." They followed her into the spacious kitchen.

Ben saw the way her narrow gaze speared him. His mother had questions, and he would be answering them before he was allowed to go to bed.

His father was sitting with Nathaniel when the small group entered the kitchen. The older man's gaze flew to where Sadie was standing. Although he didn't exclaim like his wife had, Ben could see the discomfort on his father's face.

His father, however, was a kind man, and one who took hospitality seriously.

"Benjamin. I'm happy you came home for a visit. Nathaniel here was telling me about your adventure with your friend. Sadie, *jah*?"

Abram Mast stood and made his way across the room to them.

"Yes, sir. I'm Sadie. I'm sorry to intrude on you like this."

"*Nee*, it is never an intrusion to see our son. I am interested in hearing the full story."

There was no mistaking the trepidation in Sadie's lovely eyes. To her credit, though, she smiled and nodded to his parents.

"Come," his mother said, setting a couple of plates on the table. "We have eaten, but there is plenty left."

It had been too long since he had sat and ate his mother's cooking. The talk that ensued while the meal was consumed was general in nature. His parents gave him plenty of significant looks, though.

Ben sighed. He was definitely in for a long talk with his parents. They would wait until Nathaniel and Sadie were in bed for the night. Judging by the way Nathaniel appeared to be nodding off at the table, it wouldn't be long until that happened. He wasn't surprised when Nathaniel went to bed less than fifteen minutes later. He practically had to carry him to his room. He helped him with his clothes and tucked him in under the covers. Nathaniel was growing so fast. When was the last time he'd needed such help? Smoothing his hand over his son's hair, he whispered a quiet goodnight.

Nathaniel didn't respond. He was already asleep.

In the kitchen, Ben found that his parents and a weary-eyed Sadie had waited for him. He wished she could go rest, but he knew her enough to know that she would want to be part of the conversation that had to happen. Knew that in her mind she was somehow at fault for all that had happened. He didn't believe that. She had been a victim, even more than he and Nathaniel had been. It was made worse by the fact that she had no memories to give her some clarity.

Haltingly, they began telling the story.

"I remember the cave," Abram murmured, his face pale after hearing how close he had been to losing his son and grandson. "You must have walked five miles today."

"At least," Ben agreed. "There was nothing else to

do. I know that the man we were being chased by would have found us if we had returned to my home."

"Do you think he'll come here?" Esther Mast asked.

Across the table from him, Sadie flinched. He wished he had sat beside her, but knew he was better off where he was. It aroused less suspicion. It didn't stop the longing, though. Longing that he should not be feeling.

He pushed it aside. He could not become distracted. His full attention needed to be on the current situation. Too much was at stake for him to allow this attraction he was beginning to feel to get in his way.

"I cannot promise you he won't. But I think he believes he killed us today." A shudder worked its way through him. "If he had any idea we had survived and escaped, or if he knew about the other exit, I think he would have been waiting for us. Or come after us."

"I will understand if you don't want me here," Sadie said, facing her hosts. "I'm not part of your community. You don't owe me anything."

Her face was calm, but Ben was sure her hands were clenched together under the table.

"Ach, you are a young woman in trouble." Esther's eyes narrowed in on Sadie's face again. "But you can't stay here dressed in your *Englisch* clothes."

Ben blinked. Even his father looked startled. Dressing an outsider in Amish clothes was something that was not normally done.

"Mamm?"

His mother nodded. "*Jah*, you heard me. Tomorrow morning, I will find you something to wear. If you blend in, it will harder to find you."

Sadie's eyes filled with tears, but she fought them back. He could see the muscle working in her throat as she worked to control her emotions before speaking.

"Thank you. I appreciate it. But I'm serious. If having me here puts your family at risk, I'll leave."

Abram smiled at her, although his gaze was troubled. "Whatever happens, we must remember *Gott* is in control. Always."

Whatever else might have been said was cut off as Sadie yawned. Her hand covered her mouth, but she couldn't hide it. Ben hid a grin as her eyes widened and a blush washed up her face, turning her pale complexion red.

His mother bustled into action. "Ben, you are in the room next to Nathaniel's. Come, Sadie. I will put you in the guest room on the lower level. It should be comfortable, and you should sleep tomorrow morning as late as you need to. You have had a difficult time."

His mother was gone with Sadie in a flash, leaving him staring at the doorway they'd just swept through. His father chuckled at his expression.

"*Mamm* is a wonder. *Dat*, I appreciate your help. I know that our appearance was sudden."

"I meant what I said, Ben. I am a little concerned about the attachment I sense between you and the young woman." There was no judgment, only caution.

Ben sighed. His father had always been observant.

"We are friends, *jah*? Nothing more. I will not allow it to become more. She is not Amish, although I suspect she might have been once."

Keeping his voice low, he told his father about the small pieces of memory she'd had.

"If she was Plain, she's not now." His father's words were heavy.

"I know, *Dat*."

He left his father a few moments later and made his way up to his room. He stood before the window for a few minutes, staring out into the darkness while he thought about the recent events.

Was Mason Green aware that they had survived? Unless he'd gone back into the cave to check, Ben didn't think he would have any reason to suspect that his explosion hadn't killed them. Even if it hadn't, he was bound to think that they would die buried in the cave. Hopefully he would remain unaware that they had escaped. At least long enough for the police to catch up with him.

If he found them here, there was nowhere else they could hide.

TEN

The next morning, the sun was out, bursting through the trees and lighting up the house as it streamed in through the windows. It seemed incredible that such a gorgeous day would follow one that had been filled with terror and pain.

Ben had gone out before sunrise to help his father with the morning chores. Then he remained outside for another half hour to walk around. He told his father he was going for a walk to enjoy the uncommonly mild weather. But, in truth, he was really searching for any signs that Mason Green was about.

He relaxed when he found none. Ambling back into the house, he hung his hat up on the rack inside the door and then followed his nose into the kitchen.

His *mamm* had set the breakfast on the table. Coffee, strong and black the way he liked it, percolated on the stove. Helping his *mamm* was a pretty woman dressed in a demure lavender dress that fell to midcalf. An apron was wrapped around her slender waist and plain boots were on her feet. A white prayer *kapp* covered her light brown hair. Hair he had gotten used to seeing pulled back in a ponytail.

Sadie.

His heartbeat was heavy inside his chest. This was not a good idea. How was he supposed to keep the fact that she was *Englisch* straight in his mind when she was attired in Amish clothing? Even worse was the fact that she wore it with a naturalness that stunned him. There was no self-consciousness as she worked. No fidgeting with the *kapp*. She did play with the strings that fell past her shoulders, but that was the extent of it.

The feeling that she had once been a member of a community like this grew firmer.

She wasn't a member now, and once her full memory returned she would go back to the *Englisch* world. He had to keep that in the forefront of his mind. Otherwise, he could find himself in an emotional bind that would cause suffering all around.

"Sadie! You look like us." Nathaniel rushed into the room, skidding to a stop at her side. He grinned up at the woman, and she smiled back.

"I know. Would you like some breakfast?"

Like everything was normal. Shaking his head to clear it, Ben approached the table. He did his best to keep from staring at her throughout the meal. It took some discipline. She looked so right standing in the large, open Amish kitchen working next to his mother. It wasn't hard to imagine her working with Nathaniel on his homework. Or riding in the front of the buggy with him.

Nee. He could not go there. It made the very heart

inside his chest ache to know that he must deny himself the pleasure of even considering courting her. It was the way it had to be. He felt guilty, too. The idea that he was thinking of a woman besides Lydia with longing— it couldn't continue. He knew that his parents wanted him to move on, but they would be disappointed if they knew the direction his thoughts were taking.

He needed to avoid Sadie as much as possible.

He managed to stay out of the house most of the day. When he returned in the late afternoon, however, he saw that Sadie was sitting on the porch steps peeling potatoes. He couldn't just walk past her. When she raised her hand, potato and all, and waved, he gave in. If he changed direction and went around to go in the back door, she'd know he was avoiding her.

Holding in a sigh, he strode to the porch and sat on the top step, being sure to keep the bucket between them.

"How was your day?"

She grinned. "It was a good day. Your mother is great. She told me some stories about you and your siblings. I didn't know you have four sisters."

"*Jah.* I am the youngest. My sisters have all married and have families of their own. One day, my parents hope that one of us kids will move into this haus. Then they will move into the *dawdi haus.* That's the smaller *haus* over there." He pointed to the building situated a little back from the road. He pulled something out of his pocket of his trousers and held it out to her. It was her cell phone. "I had this charged at my *dat's* shop this morning. I thought since you are *Englisch*, you should have this. Your brother or the police might try to call you."

She frowned. Not a scared or a sad frown. More of a contemplative expression.

"Thank you. I wouldn't want to offend your family by having this, but if you think it's okay." She reached over and took the phone. Their fingers brushed. He kept himself from jerking his hand away, but only just. Sadie's cheeks became rosy. Without a word, she slipped the cell phone into her apron pocket. Then her gaze flicked over to the house they had been discussing. "*Dawdi haus.* I know that term. That's the house where the grandparents live. Since you were the youngest, and the only son, I would have expected that you would have moved in."

He averted his eyes. "*Jah.* Lydia and I, we had planned to take over the farm. We lived with my parents for a few years. My *dat*, he is still plenty young to run the farm and his workshop. He's a carpenter, like me. My brother-in-law is his assistant."

It should have been him and he knew it. The pain of losing Lydia and their baby girl had been too great to stay here. That and the constant pressure to remarry. He had let the family down; he knew it, but he couldn't change the past.

She tilted her head, her keen eyes making him squirm. He had left instead of taking over. He had done what he thought was necessary for himself and for Nathaniel, but now he was having trouble dealing with the uncomfortable knowledge that he had made such a selfish decision.

"I'm sure they understood," Sadie told him, her compassion for his struggle evident.

He started. Had he said his thoughts out loud?

"How do you know what I'm thinking?" he asked her, not quite able to keep the question from sounding like a challenge. It wasn't that he was angry. He wasn't. What he was, however, was feeling exposed and vulnerable. He had not opened up to anyone about what he had suffered through when Lydia had been lost to him.

"I don't know what you're thinking." She leaned a little closer. His breath caught. Two inches closer and she'd be near enough to kiss.

Absolutely not. He stood to put some distance between them. She shrugged and began to peel the potatoes again.

"Also, you are constantly looking back at the house. A little line here," she said, touching the tip of her pinkie finger to her forehead. "I just followed the clues."

He was relieved. And, he realized, a little disappointed. If she had already known some of what was on his mind, it would give him a reason to tell her. He suddenly needed to talk about his wife's death. About the agony that had followed them since the day she was diagnosed.

He wasn't sure how to begin such a conversation.

Apparently, he waited too long. Sadie picked up the peeled potatoes and headed back inside the house, leaving him staring after her.

What was she thinking, trying to encourage Ben to talk with her about his personal business? So not smart.

He was a good man, a man she wanted to consider a friend, but she was not his confidante. She could not be that person. It was hard enough to keep her emotional distance. She knew that he felt the attraction. Or, at least, she thought he did.

But it was absolutely never going to be more than that. She needed to stop herself before she fell head-long into heartbreak and led a good man there with her.

Her pocket vibrated.

What?

She stopped and placed her hand in her apron pocket. She had already forgotten about the cell phone that Ben had handed her earlier. Nathaniel and Esther were laughing together in the kitchen. She didn't want to disturb them. It didn't feel polite to pull it out in the middle of the house, so she strode quickly to the room Esther had shown her to and closed the door. Heart racing, she pulled the phone out and unlocked the screen.

She froze. Kurt's number was on the screen. She had missed the call from him, but he had left a message.

Or someone using his phone had left a message.

Suddenly, she didn't want to listen to the message alone. Not giving herself time to question her actions, she fled the house and went in search of Ben. If the message was bad, he was the one person she knew could help, the one person she knew she could trust.

Making sure that Nathaniel was still occupied with his grandmother, she stepped quietly out the door. She wasn't quite sure where she should go to find Ben. It struck her that she should try his father's carpentry shop first. That seemed to be a logical assumption. Ben was not a man who liked to be idle. Therefore, it made sense that he would have wanted to go and help his father while they were staying with them.

Having a focus, she walked briskly across the grass and up the path to where Abram Mast had set up his shop. When she got to the door, she paused for a moment. Did she knock? Or was it acceptable to just enter? Biting her lip, she knocked softly on the glass pane of the door. She waited. When no one came to answer the door, she knocked a little louder. Almost immediately, the door opened, and she was relieved to come face-to-face with the man she had been looking for.

A little too happy to find him. She felt the sudden urge to walk across the threshold and hug him. That's when she knew that she was really rattled by the missed phone call. She checked her motion just in time. Rather than moving forward as she wished, she forced herself to take a step back, away from him.

Nonplussed, Ben stopped and stared at her. He had no clue how close he had come to being embraced. She felt the warmth in her cheeks, but decided she had more pressing issues than her near faux pas.

"Can you talk for a moment?" She folded her arms across her middle, striving to keep all her suppressed tension and concern down inside.

"*Jah*. Wait here a moment." He turned back and walked to his father. She could hear the two men holding a low-voiced conversation, but it was too quiet for her to understand what they were saying. Sadie grimaced. They were probably talking in Pennsylvania Dutch, the term used to describe the dialect of German used by the Amish. She was almost glad that she couldn't hear it. It was starting to unnerve her a little bit just how much of the language she seemed to understand. Her brother had given her no indication that she had ever spent any kind of extended time with Amish people before. So where did she learn it?

This was a question she needed an answer to, but maybe right now wasn't the time to explore it. Her brother needed her.

Ben joined her at the door, then gestured that she should lead the way. She had no idea where they could go.

"Maybe we could just walk around for a few minutes. I don't want to go inside because I don't want your folks or Nathaniel to hear."

His brows lowered, letting her know he was a little disturbed by her words. But he nodded. She waited until they were far enough from the buildings that she felt comfortable that no one would be able to tell what they were saying. Keeping her back facing the buildings, she drew her phone out of her pocket of her apron.

"I was inside and I felt my phone vibrate." She watched his expression as she spoke. "I had missed a call from Kurt. Actually, I should say that I missed a call from his phone. I have no idea if he was the one who really called me. The last time I called him, someone else answered it. Whoever it was, they left a voice mail message."

"Why didn't you listen to the message?" His words were gruff, at odds with the concerned expression on his face.

"I'm scared to listen to it." It wasn't easy to admit this weakness, but she felt he would understand. "At least, alone. I have no idea what this message will say. I am imagining all sorts of horrible things."

He stepped closer to her than was absolutely appropriate. A comforting hand settled on her shoulder. "I'm here with you. I know you're scared, but we will listen to this message together."

She nodded. She touched her phone to unlock it, but paused.

"Can we— Do you think—"

"What do you need?"

She pursed her lips and blew out a breath. "Could we pray?"

She could hardly believe those words were coming out of her mouth, but they seemed like the right words to say. Ben's face lit up with surprise, his eyes flared wide and his brows shot up. Then he smiled.

"*Jah*. We will pray and ask *Gott* for His guidance and help."

Gratitude welled up within her. Then he bowed his head and she copied his pose.

"*Gott*, You alone know what will come today and the day after that. You alone know the future and know what is truly in our hearts. We ask You to be with us, to guide us and to help us bring Kurt home and to help us all be safe."

When he said amen, Sadie echoed it, feeling a little awkward, but at the same time there was a sense of peace.

It was time. Clenching her teeth together, she unlocked her phone and tapped in the four digit pass-code. Then she opened up her voice mail and put it on speaker. Hearing her brother's voice come out of the phone nearly brought her to her knees.

"Sadie, it's me. Kurt. Listen, don't call me back. I managed to steal back my phone and get away. But they're after me. I am going to try and sneak into my office. I can't let anyone see me, though. I don't know how, but I believe that my boss might be involved with whoever is after you. And the man who attacked me. I can't go into any details right now. I'm safe for the mo-ment, and if I can I will contact you later. I hope that you are with Ben. He's the one person right now that I trust to keep you safe. I don't know if you've remem-bered me yet, but I love you and I will do everything I can to finish this up and to get back to you soon. Don't take any chances."

The message ended. Without thinking about it she hit the number to save the message on her phone. Then she looked up at Ben and bit her lip.

"I saved the message, but what should we do with it? It hardly seems feasible for us to travel all the way back to the Waylan Grove Police Department. What do you think?"

For a moment he didn't say anything. She knew from the look on his face he was trying to process all that they had heard and come up with the best solution.

"I agree that I don't think we should go back to Way-lan Grove. Even dressed Plain like you are, you could still be recognized. Mason Green has seen me now, so he would recognize me, as well." He tugged on his ear thoughtfully. "Your brother was right. We don't know who we can trust. If his boss was responsible for leading him into a trap, who else might be involved in this? I know your brother fairly well. He has spoken of his boss, Ethan. I know that Ethan is a man that he respects and has always considered a friend. To know that such a man had betrayed him—" Ben shook his head.

Sadie thought about what he had said and her heart broke a little more for her brother. Not only because of the physical danger he was in, but because of the pain he had to be suffering emotionally.

"I'm worried, Ben. Kurt told me not to take any chances, but I think that he will. I'm so scared that he will get hurt, or worse."

He nodded. "*Jah*, I know what you are saying. We will keep praying. And we will do everything we can to help the police find the people responsible for this."

They continued to walk for a few minutes, allowing the silence to settle between them. It was a comfortable silence, one filled with mutual care and concern. Sadie knew that no matter what else happened, she could depend on Ben.

She also knew that as soon as this whole debacle was finished, she would sever ties with him. Not because of anything he'd done. But because if she didn't sever ties with him, she didn't know if she would ever be able to see another man without comparing him to Ben.

The steady *clop, clop, clop* of horse hooves trotting down the road in front of the house caught her attention. Her curiosity grew when the buggy pulled by a chestnut mare with a white blaze on her forehead turned and headed up the driveway. The driver halted the horse, bounded off the seat of the buggy and headed over to where she was standing with Ben.

She turned to her companion. His mouth had fallen open, and joy and astonishment were battling for ownership on his face. This was no average visitor. Whoever this was coming toward them, it was someone who meant a lot to Ben.

"Isaac? Isaac Yoder?" Ben breathed.

Immediately her heart started to beat wildly within her chest. Isaac Yoder. Ben Mast.

She had been wrong. She did know the Amish. Not only that, she knew these Amish.

ELEVEN

"Ben Mast!" In seconds, Isaac was standing before them, a wide grin spreading across his bearded face. His blue eyes sparkled with pleasure. "Your father told me you were home. I couldn't believe it. I haven't seen you in years!"

Sadie looked up at Ben. His grin was easily a match for Isaac's. If she wasn't mistaken, his eyes had a sudden sheen to them. He blinked and it was gone.

"You can't believe I'm home?" Ben laughed out loud. "You're the one who left the Amish community altogether to go live with the *Englisch*. I only moved to a new area."

"I did. It's true. I didn't think I would ever come back." Isaac's grin widened. "Nor that I would find a lovely Amish girl who would be willing to marry me. Then I met my Lizzy. And here I am."

"*Jah*, here we both are. You seem happy."

"I am. God is good."

That brought out another grin. This time, she thought that Ben looked like he'd been handed a gift. Had Isaac

lost his faith at one point? It was possible, since he'd
left. She couldn't get over the fact that she was again
with these two, and they had no clue who she really was.
Her throat clogged. She didn't know if she'd be able to
talk, emotion was choking her so hard.

The two men seem to realize that they were leaving
Sadie out of the conversation. Isaac turned to her with
his easy grin.

"I'm sorry. I knew you had a guest, Ben."

"Ack! I am being so rude. My apologies, Sadie. This
is my old friend—"

He never finished his sentence. It was too much for
Sadie. The emotions that she had been holding back
came spilling out of her all at once. The tears streamed
down her cheeks and the sob that she had been trying to
stifle burst free. Ben's astonished face swam before her
eyes briefly before she covered her face with her hands.

"Sadie?" She heard the confusion in Ben's voice. She
struggled to answer.

"I remember, Ben," she managed to choke out.

Shocked, Ben stared at her. Isaac's face had gone
flat. Not angry or disgusted. Observant. The face of
someone used to facing hard situations and making
quick decisions.

"Let's get you inside." Before she knew it, Ben was
urging her back toward the house.

"Maybe... Should I leave?" Isaac asked.

"Nee!" she said, the Amish word for *no* slipping past
her lips instinctively. She ignored it. There was so much
going on inside her at the moment, she could not focus

on anything other than her recovered memories. "You need to come. You have to hear this."

Distractedly, she was aware of the look that flashed between the two men, but was too distraught to think much of it. Memories were bombarding her from all sides. Memories of being held in a woman's lap while the buggy they were in swayed back and forth. Where had they been going? She had no idea. She had other memories. Memories of baking cookies with an older woman. Her grandmother? She couldn't be sure, but she thought so.

Again and again the images came. They came at her so fast she was having trouble processing them. At one point, she closed her eyes and let Ben lead her. She stumbled once but regained her balance when he caught her around the waist.

"Easy, Sadie. I have you. Just a little farther." Ben continued to support her as the trio walked. Isaac kept his thoughts to himself. She couldn't imagine what was going through his mind right then.

Then they were in the house, and he was leading her to a chair in the living room. His mother came out of the kitchen, wiping her hands on a dish towel. When she saw the tears on Sadie's cheeks, she rushed forward, making clicking noises with her tongue.

"What's this? What has happened?" She edged herself in next to Sadie, squeezing Ben out of the way. Ben caught himself before he could trip, then he moved to stand on Sadie's other side. A giggle burbled up inside her, turning into a sob before she could get it out. Her vision blurred as more tears tumbled down. Sadie brushed them away impatiently. She hated crying. She'd done more in the past week than she had in a long time.

"She said she was remembering," Ben explained to his mother.

Compassion filled her eyes. She placed her warm, motherly hand on Sadie's cold one. "Dear child. What did you remember? Can you tell us?"

She nodded. With an effort, she calmed herself and drew in a deep breath. "I—I remember sitting on my mother's lap. I'm pretty sure it was my mother. We were going someplace but I don't know where. I could feel the swaying motion as we traveled." She looked up at Ben. He was her focal point. His warm eyes held on to hers, almost like an embrace. She was not alone. Focusing on him helped her to continue. "I think we were in a buggy."

Ben did not look surprised. "I wondered if you had spent some time with the Amish."

That got her attention. "What made you wonder such a thing?"

Ben moved a little apart from her and settled himself on the chair across the way. He leaned forward and rested his arms on his knees. "Several times you have used our language without even thinking about it. Which told me that you had some experience speaking it. Of course, that did not prove anything. It could have meant a number of things. Maybe you had Amish friends. You worked in a school. Oftentimes, we have Amish children with special needs who attend public school with the *Englisch* kids. There were other things, too. You told me yourself how you seemed to remember cooking certain foods with Ruth. Remember that?"

She nodded. She'd forgotten all about that in the panic of the past few days. But he hadn't. She wondered briefly what else he remembered about her.

"Wow. Yes, I do remember that."

"I also noticed that you seem to have knowledge of certain traditions that we have. It made sense to me that you had a deep connection with the Amish at some point in your life but you didn't remember it."

Esther broke in. "Your mother, do you remember her?"

"Yes. I do remember her. And I remember how devastated I was when she and my stepfather were killed in a fire two years ago." She grabbed onto Esther's hands. "I don't remember very much before I was seven years old. I do know that something happened and I was pretty traumatized for a while. I remember not speaking for a long time. Once I started speaking again, my mom and I never talked about what had happened. I do remember that I asked her about my life before, but she would just shake her head and say that some things needed to be forgotten. She always got this look on her face that scared me a bit. I stopped asking. So I'm still missing a chunk of my life. But I have some images."

Esther frowned, but nodded. Sadie could tell that the older woman was disappointed. She didn't need to think very hard about why. She remembered Esther's comments to her on the day that they met. How well had Esther known Hannah Bontrager? Had they been friends?

"My mother," she whispered to the older woman. "Her name was Hannah. Hannah Bontrager. And she was Amish."

Tears brightened Esther's eyes. A smile wobbled on her lips. It was a smile filled with grief. "I knew it."

"Mamm?"

Sadie and Esther both turned to see that Ben had half risen from his seat. No doubt he was concerned that seeing his mother brought tears.

"Shush, Ben. It's all right."

Sadie looked between Isaac and Ben. How could she not have remembered? She was swamped again by bittersweet emotions. Happiness at having her memories back, regret at having missed so much.

"Sadie, why am I here?" Isaac asked her. She could tell it wasn't a rude question. She had specifically told him she needed both him and Ben to be there when she went over what she was remembering.

"My childhood is a blur for the most part. But there are a couple things that I do remember. I told you how I remembered my mother. I also remember playing games and following my two best friends, Ben Mast and Isaac Yoder, around everywhere we went."

Both men's mouths dropped open, shocked, as they listened to the words tumbling from her.

"Sadie Ann Bontrager." The hoarse words dropped from his lips. Ben probably didn't even realize that he had spoken her name aloud.

She nodded in confirmation of her identity. "Yes. I was eight when my mother remarried. I remember that my last name was Bontrager, and my stepfather adopted me and gave me his last name. My mother told me I needed to never again call myself Sadie Bontrager. In fact, she strongly warned me to forget my last name. I had wondered why, but she was so stern, I never questioned it."

"You disappeared. One day you were there and the next day you were gone," Ben mused, his gaze sharp on her face. Isaac's eyes were on the floor.

She nodded, watching them piece together the information.

Isaac suddenly jerked upright, his face intent. "Your father—"

Ben paled. "The flashback you had, the one about seeing the Amish man murdered?"

She already didn't like where this was going. But she had wondered the same thing. Knowing in her heart what the answer was, she asked the question they were all thinking.

"He was my father, wasn't he?" She had no memories of him other than that image, but she knew deep within her soul that she was right. Ben's slow nod confirmed it. New anguish spread through her.

"He was murdered, and a young teenager was sent to jail. Two days later, you were gone."

"You weren't just raised in an Amish community," Ben said. "You were raised in *this* Amish community."

"I don't think you can say that I was raised here. I lived here until I was around seven, then I left. And we never looked back. Until all of this happened, I had forgotten completely about my Amish past."

"Wow." Isaac sank into a chair. "Sadie Bontrager. I don't even know what to say. Just wow."

That surprised a laugh out of her. He sounded so *Englisch* when he said that, his years away from the Amish showing. Ben chuckled, too, although it was a little strained.

Isaac collected himself and looked at Sadie. "I won't get into the whole story, because it's not important right now. But I will tell you that when I left the Amish community, I spent several years working as a cop for the Waylan Grove Police Department."

Hearing that Isaac used to be a cop surprised Ben. Although maybe not so much. He remembered the fight Isaac had had with his father after his brother, Joshua, had been killed. Isaac had been all about finding justice. So maybe joining the police force had been his way to do that.

A thought struck him. "Isaac, did you work with a Sergeant Ryder Howard?"

Isaac laughed lightly. "Ryder? Sure. He's a buddy of mine. He made sergeant just last spring. He has one of my dogs."

Ben didn't quite understand that. "One of your dogs?"

"Yeah. I had gotten into raising service dogs and training them to be K-9 officers. When I rejoined the community, the bishop told me I could keep training the dogs. Well, he gave me permission to train service dogs. I don't train them for K-9 cop work anymore. The one I had trained, I gave to Ryder. It's made him quite the envy of the other officers."

"I'm sure." Ben shook his head, amused in spite of the seriousness of the conversation.

The humor drained out of Isaac's face. "Seriously. He's a good guy. And he's an outstanding cop. I trust him completely."

"Ben, we should tell him about the voice mail."

Ben had almost forgotten about the message. "*Mamm*, could you excuse us for a few minutes?"

Ben rose, and Isaac and Sadie followed suit. This was not something he wanted to discuss while his mother was in the room. He led the others out onto the front porch. After he had shut the door firmly behind him, he looked at Sadie.

Interpreting his look correctly, she pulled her cell phone out of her apron and replayed the message for Isaac. The former police officer listened to the message without speaking. When the message was finished however, he questioned the both of them thoroughly.

"What do you think?" Ben ask him.

"I think we should call Ryder and set up a meeting."

"I'm not sure going back to Waylan Grove would be a wise decision for us."

Ben and Sadie took turns explaining everything that had happened the past few days. Again Isaac listened.

"I understand you not wanting to go back there. Let me contact Ryder and see if he will come here. I'm also curious about this boss of Kurt's. What was his name? Ethan? What do you know about him?"

Sadie tugged at the strings of her *kapp*. "I only met

him once, a couple of weeks before the accident. Kurt had invited him and his wife to dinner one night. His wife was nice enough. Didn't talk a lot. Something about him made me uncomfortable, but I didn't know why."

"Last name?"

She shook her head. "I'm sorry. I really don't know. Kurt always referred to him as Ethan."

"I'll contact Ryder," Isaac decided. "Then when he shows up, we can decide where we go from here."

"We?" Ben and Sadie chorused.

Isaac scoffed and cast him a scathing glance. "What? Do you expect me to stay out of this? In a single day I have recovered two of my best childhood friends. Friends that I had thought I would never see again. There's no way I'm walking away from this. The way I figure it, God must have wanted us to meet up again. Who am I to disagree with Him?"

"*Denke,*" Ben said, touched more than he could say. There had been so many times in the past three years when he had felt isolated and alone. He had people in the community where he lived whom he liked. Caleb and Lovina, for instance. But he really didn't have anyone that he shared a strong bond of friendship with. He hadn't truly felt that bond for a long time. Isaac was right.

"Who are we to disagree, indeed."

Isaac left a few minutes later, promising to bring his wife by to meet them soon. "You'll like my Lizzy. She's from a little town in Pennsylvania. We met when I was a cop."

Intrigued, Ben raised an eyebrow. "She met you while you were Fancy?"

Isaac rolled his eyes. "I was *Englisch*, and yes, that's when she met me. I didn't come back to being Amish because of her, though. I knew that if I came back to being Amish, it was a lifelong choice. Which meant I needed to do it for the right reasons. It would not have been fair to her to join the church and then not be able to truly live this life."

Would Sadie ever— Ben stamped that thought out before it fully formed. She had said she didn't remember very much about her Amish life. For all intents and purposes, she was *Englisch*. And although he could feel the tension and the bond between them growing stronger every day, he knew he didn't have the right to ask her to become anything else. Not for him.

When this was all over, when Mason Green had been caught and Sadie was out of danger, what would she choose? Would she choose to return to her roots, or would she go back to her old job and her old way of life?

He was getting far too invested in her choices. He had a son to think about. He already knew that Nathaniel loved Sadie. Just as he was growing to love… *Nee*. That was not possible. They had not known each other long enough for him to truly love her.

He decided it was best if he ignored the idea.

But it didn't matter. A hollow spot had opened up inside him and it had Sadie's name on it. Soon she'd be gone.

Whatever was building between the two of them needed to end. Now.

TWELVE

Early the next day, Isaac showed up after breakfast. He chatted with the Masts for a few moments before requesting to see Ben and Sadie privately. The three of them walked out to the barn. Ben had the oddest feeling, being with two friends who had both left his life for so many years. He thanked Gott for the blessing of seeing them again.

"What are we waiting for?" Ben asked.

"Ryder's coming. He has been investigating your brother's boss. Ethan Nettle. The man's record is clean. In fact, it's so clean, he doesn't even have a parking ticket. Nothing."

"And that bothers you?" Sadie asked, her voice slightly amused.

"Yeah, it does. The man drives one of those fancy cars. It's a Corvette or something like that. The ones that go a million miles per hour. Who owns a toy like that and doesn't test it out?"

Ben chuckled. "I managed to drive one during my

rumspringa. Scared me enough to make me understand the benefit of my nice sedate buggy."

They didn't have long to wait before the sound of a car pulling into the driveway reached their ears. A few seconds later, a door banged shut. Isaac peeked out of the barn. "In here, Ryder."

The officer strode up the driveway, his hard shoes clomping on the gravel as he moved. Within a minute, he entered the barn. With him came a large German shepherd, wearing a bright blue harness with the name Lily on it.

Isaac grinned. "Here's my girl. Ben, Sadie, this is Lily. The pup I trained."

Ryder snorted. "She's not a pup anymore, dude. Now she's a fully trained canine officer, aren't you, Lily?"

The dog sat when commanded to.

"Sergeant Howard," Ben began.

The officer waved his hand. "Ryder. I am really glad to see you two. After you walked out of the police station, we were all a bit anxious about your whereabouts. Isaac's phone call was a welcome one, that's for sure."

Ben felt a momentary pang of guilt over that. He hoped the officer hadn't gotten into trouble because of them. "Fine. Ryder. What have you learned about Ethan Nettle?"

Ryder leaned a shoulder against a post. "Well, that's interesting. It appears that Mr. Nettle has had some success in reporting on social justice issues. For example, he's very well-known for being a force against drug cartels and illegal human trafficking. Particularly when it comes to women and children."

Ben frowned. "I don't see how that is a bad thing. Those are both evils that our world would be better off without."

"Ah, yes, true." Ryder nodded sagely. "Trouble is, it has long been suspected that Mason Green is deeply connected to both of those markets. It has also come to my notice that quite a few times in the past ten years or so, Mason Green has been spotted in the same place where Ethan Nettle was supposedly working on reporting a story. In fact, in at least three instances, I have witnesses who could place both men in the same hotel. What do you think about that coincidence?"

"I don't believe in coincidence," Ben bit out harshly. He could think of very few things that were as evil as the victimization of children and women. If Kurt's boss was associating with these people, and in fact, profiting from this evil, he needed to be dealt with. Ben remembered Sadie being concerned that Kurt would take chances. She was probably correct. Kurt would put himself at risk to save others. Of that he had no doubt.

"Yeah, me neither." Ryder reached into his back pocket. He pulled out an envelope. When he slipped it open and took out a picture, Ben's stomach clenched. "I actually have a digital copy of this on my computer. However, I didn't know about the service out here so I printed it out so that we could all see it."

He turned to Sadie. "I need you to take a look at this and tell me what you see."

Sadie paled slightly, but she nodded and took a step closer. Her arm brushed against Ben's. He could feel her shivering beside him, and he was fairly certain it was not from the cold. Without giving it a thought, he lightly placed his arm around her shoulders. Isaac raised his eyebrow at him, but he ignored his childhood friend. Right at this moment, Sadie needed his comfort.

"Alles ist gut," he murmured in her ear. "All of us are here with you. No one will hurt you."

"I know," she whispered. "I'm just a little nervous. I can't believe that my brother has been working with this man all these years and has never had a clue. What if Kurt had somehow stumbled onto what he was up to? Who knows what Ethan would've done?"

Ben didn't want to respond to that because he had a fairly good idea of what the man would have done. His arm tightened slightly as Ryder showed Sadie the photograph.

She gasped and swayed slightly.

Instinctively, Ben pulled her closer. She leaned against him for a moment, then she stood straight. He let her go, even though it pained him. She pointed to the red-headed man sitting at the table in a café. "That's my brother's boss, Ethan. And the other man, the one he's sitting with as if they were old friends, that's Mason Green."

She shuddered once, then she looked up at Ben. He saw the anguish in her eyes. "You've remembered something else, haven't you?"

He felt more than saw both Isaac and Ryder straighten. She kept her eyes locked with his. He silently urged her to keep going, knowing that all of this was taking its toll.

"That night my brother had Ethan and his wife over to dinner, they were talking about a story that Kurt was working on. He hadn't told me what it was. I was still pretty torn up because a young girl from the school I work at had been kidnapped and later found in very bad shape. I think it's connected but I'm not sure yet. I didn't mean to eavesdrop, but we have a small house with thin walls. I could hear Kurt trying to convince Ethan to let him write a story. He said he had found some interesting clues and a witness who could prove that someone he was looking into was, in fact, involved in something pretty nasty. I didn't hear what it was, but looking back it was obviously illegal human trafficking. Anyway, Ethan said no. Oh, he was very nice about it. Very complimentary about my brother. My brother did such great work but they just didn't have room for that kind of story at this moment. Maybe later on down the line. I knew for a fact that my brother was anxious to get his hands on a meatier story. He had been researching this angle for so long, just waiting to pitch it to his boss. But Ethan wasn't buying it. I felt bad for my brother but what could I do? I have no knowledge of journalism. I had no idea what would be a good story, or how to even go about finding one."

She turned to look at Ryder and Isaac. "But I had no clue there was anything more going on. Later that evening, I walked into the little office that my brother and I shared. I had a knitting pattern that I wanted to show Ethan's wife. I can't even remember the woman's name at this point. It doesn't matter. Anyway, I knocked some papers off my brother's desk. When I bent down to pick them up, I saw a picture. It was a picture of Mason Green. I believe he was the man that my brother was researching. Anyway, as I looked at the picture, I had a flashback."

Ben could tell she was getting very agitated. Whatever she had remembered, it must've been horrible.

"Can you tell us, Sadie?" Ryder asked, his voice gentle. Ben was a very peaceful man, but he felt a small spurt of anger at the officer for putting even the tiniest bit of pressure on Sadie. He held it in, though, knowing the man was only doing his job. And also knowing that until Mason Green and Ethan Nettle were caught, Sadie would never be safe again.

Sadie drew in a deep breath. "I remember being a child. I was only six or seven. I was outside, it was a warm summer day. I remember a man grabbing me and trying to throw me into his car. It was Mason Green. He couldn't have been that old. Late teens? Knowing what I know now, I believe he was intending to kidnap me."

Her words sent a chill straight through him. There was only one reason Mason Green would have tried to kidnap a young Amish girl. He had planned to sell her in the human trafficking market.

"What happened?" Ben felt like each word was a chip of ice spewing from his mouth.

Tears welled up in those beautiful caramel-colored eyes and rolled down her cheeks.

"My father stopped him."

She took the handkerchief from Ben's hand and wiped her face. Her story wasn't done. She needed to keep it together for a few more minutes.

"My father heard me screaming. He came out and

saw what was happening. He rushed over and grabbed me from Mason's arms. He threw me away from him, and when I looked at him, Mason Green was holding a gun to my father. Before I could do anything, he shot him. Right in front of me. I think between my screaming and the shot, several people on the street came out to see what was happening. Mason threw the gun down and took off. One of our neighbors, a teenager from a non-Amish family, was first on the scene. He was about fifteen or so and had a reputation for getting in trouble."

"He picked up the gun, didn't he?" Ben asked. He remembered very well the day that Sadie's father was killed. He also remembered running out of his house and seeing an older boy holding the gun.

"He did. I was in such shock that I didn't realize what was happening. There were no witnesses other than myself to say that he was innocent. He was literally holding the smoking gun in his hand. I shut down for a while. Mentally. And after that, it was like my mind had closed the memory away. I literally didn't remember what had happened. Until now."

"You can't blame yourself for what happened, Sadie." Isaac's face was so sad as he looked at his friend. "It's horrible. But you were a child."

She nodded to show she understood, but the grief inside her was overwhelming. She had blocked the memory out for so long, she felt that she was only now starting to grieve her father. And that poor kid who went to jail.

"His name was Jeffrey, I think."

"I need you to write your statement out and sign it.

There's no statute of limitations on murder. If you give us your statement, it means we can go before the judge, ask for Jeffrey to be released and for the case of the murder of your father to be opened up again."

She thought, *But Amish don't usually give statements or testify*, then rolled her eyes. She hadn't been Amish for a very long time. And there was no one left who could help.

Decision made, she nodded her affirmative. "I'll do whatever I must to help."

Ryder rubbed his hands together in anticipation. "Great! I am so glad that you're going to do this." He hesitated. "Um, today would be good."

"Today? As in, right now?" The idea of leaving and going back to Waylan Grove now, when things were still so up in the air, made her stomach churn. What if Mason Green was still out there searching for them? And now that she knew about Ethan Nettle, there were at least two people trying to kill her. It didn't seem the wisest decision to go back into the middle of the fray alone.

We are never alone.

Suddenly, that peace she had felt once before spread through her. She knew what it meant. Even if it was just her going into battle, God was with her. She needed to rely on him and not on her own strength. Not even on Ben's strength. Because even though Ben was just about the best man she had ever met, he was still a man. Only God was perfect. Only God could truly save her.

"I'll go," she told Ryder.

"Let me tell *Dat* that I won't be here to help this

afternoon," Ben announced. "I'm sure my *mamm* would be willing to watch out for Nathaniel while we're gone. She's enjoying having a grandchild in the house."

Surprised, she glanced at him. "You're coming with me?"

He snorted. "*Jah*. Absolutely I'm going with you. Did you think I would leave you to face this danger by yourself?"

"Hey," Ryder protested. "I'm here, too, you know. I'd not let her go by herself."

As he'd predicted, Ben's parents agreed to keep Nathaniel while he accompanied Ryder and Sadie back to Waylan Grove. To her further surprise, as they approached the police cruiser, Isaac hopped into the front seat, leaving the back seat to Sadie and Ben. And Lily. The large dog hopped up beside Sadie and calmly settled on the leather seat.

Sadie felt like she had swallowed rocks for lunch, and now they were sitting heavy in her stomach. She placed her hand over her belly, trying to still the churning going on inside her. The scenery whizzed past. She almost missed the slower pace of the buggy. When you were in a buggy, you could really appreciate the places you were driving past.

The closer they came to Waylan Grove, the tighter her nerves became. She nearly jumped out of her skin when a warm hand landed on top of hers where it was lying on the seat. Startled, she jerked her eyes up. Her gaze collided with Ben's.

"Are you well?" he whispered, concern shining from his face.

Her immediate reaction was to say she was fine. But she wasn't fine. She was far from it. Right at the moment, she didn't want to placate anyone with white lies designed to make them feel better. She wanted to be honest.

"No, I'm really not. I'm learning to trust God, but it's still so hard to understand how anyone could do evil things to another person. And I am so worried about Kurt. All he ever wanted was to make a difference. And now he's stuck in the middle of this mess. It's not fair."

"*Jah.* I know it's not fair. If I could change the situation and make it better for you, I would. But I will not leave you until the situation has been resolved."

And after that? But she knew better than to ask. Ben was an honorable man, but he was still not the man for her.

When they arrived in Waylan Grove, the crowded police cruiser pulled into the station parking lot and Ryder backed into a space. As soon as the doors were unlocked, all four of its human passengers and Lily spilled out into the afternoon light. Sadie sniffed the air. Nearby, someone was burning leaves. She could also smell the faint scent of fresh bread coming from the bakery across the street. Her stomach rumbled. They'd have to get some food after this. She would never make it all the way back to Ben's parents' house without eating again. It would have been nice if they could have waited until after lunch, but they were already here.

Ryder led the small group into the same conference room that she had been in just a few days before. He gave her some paper and a pen and told her to write down her statement. Never having done such a thing, she was unsure how to go about it.

"Just write down everything you can remember," he told her. That was a lot.

Sighing, she bent her head and started. She had no idea how long it took her to get the entire statement written, but her fingers felt cramped by the time she was done. Hopefully, this would be enough to get Jeffrey out of prison. And hopefully her statement would be enough to get the real criminals locked behind bars for the rest of their lives.

She signed her name with a flourish and set down her pen. "Done."

Ryder took her statement. "I have an impromptu appointment with the district attorney. I shouldn't be long."

Her stomach growled again, embarrassing her.

"If it's all right with you, I think I will take Sadie down the street to that restaurant we passed. Neither of us had a chance to eat lunch, and I think we're both in need of some nourishment."

"Perfect. What are you gonna do, Isaac?"

He hesitated.

"You are more than welcome to come with us," she told him sincerely. "I doubt you had a chance to eat, either."

He considered it and finally agreed. "I might as well. I don't have anything to do here. It just feels strange, being in the station and not actually working here."

The three of them headed over to the restaurant. It was one of those places where they could either sit down inside or they could order what they wanted from the take-out menu and have it boxed up to go.

"I don't know that eating in a restaurant would be comfortable right now," she told her companions. "I would be constantly looking around to see if there was any danger."

"*Jah*, that would not be relaxing. Let's grab some food and then we can go back over to the station to eat it," Ben recommended.

Within fifteen minutes they all had their bags of freshly cooked food. The aromas of garlic and butter were too tempting to resist. As they crossed the street, Sadie dipped her hand into her bag and brought out a cheesy breadstick. "I love these things."

She bit into one. The delicious flavors of warm cheese, garlic and butter burst on her tongue. She had forgotten how much she enjoyed Italian cuisine.

The gunshot came out of nowhere, or so it seemed. She had just swallowed another bite of the breadstick when a loud crack split the air, followed immediately by a crash as the window she had just passed by smashed to pieces.

Screams filled the air. The car that was stopped at the red light at the intersection suddenly revved hard. Horns honked in annoyance as the driver cut off those who were coming from the opposite direction. One of the cars slammed on its brakes to avoid a collision. The car behind it tried to stop, but ended up with its hood crunching against the first car's bumper.

It was chaos. The car that had run the red light sped around the corner. As the driver turned, he pointed a gun directly at her. For one frozen second, she stared into the cold, deadly gaze of Mason Green. The memory of his trying to kidnap her as a child sprang fresh into her mind.

"Sadie! Get down!" Ben grabbed onto her and threw her to the ground as the second bullet erupted from the barrel of the pistol. She hit the concrete, hard, but the bullet whizzed past them.

Sirens blared as a police cruiser raced from the station and tore off after the car Mason Green had been driving. Within seconds, both vehicles had vanished from sight. Other officers were at the intersection, helping the two cars that had collided. Fortunately, she could see both drivers milling around as the police took statements, so they must not have been injured.

She sat up, dazed. Frantically, her eyes roamed over to Ben and Isaac, searching for any signs that they had been injured.

Seeing none, her shoulders sagged.

Then they tightened up again. "Ben!"

"What?" He was right beside her again. She had scared him, she could tell by the pallor of his face.

"He recognized me. Even in Amish clothes, he knew it was me. Which means he knows I'm not dead."

Ben's face set. "He must have spotted us on our way into town."

If they didn't catch him now, how long would it be before he discovered her hiding place and came after her there?

THIRTEEN

Ben waited for Ryder to finish his discussion with the chief. For once, standing still came as a challenge to him. He paced the confines of the conference room. Isaac was with Ryder, hoping to move things along.

His poor Sadie was exhausted.

He stopped, shaken. She was not his Sadie. He couldn't even begin to think that way. And yet he was. Even after all the warnings he had given himself to keep his distance, he had fallen in love with the lovely young woman sitting so desolately at the table. He had been by her side, but she had informed him that his nervous energy was making her tired.

A total role reversal.

She was so quiet, she was making him worried. What was going on in her mind? With all the things she'd remembered today and then to be shot at. It had to be devastating.

He wanted to go home and see his son.

Nee, more than that. He wanted to take Sadie back to his parents' house and know that she was safe. Being in the police station was making him impatient. Although it was unlikely that Mason Green or Ethan Nettle would be bold enough to come inside to attack.

In his mind he again heard the crack of the bullet and relived the moment when he'd thought Sadie had been shot. He'd been ready to jump in front of the gun for her. When she hit the cement, she'd dropped so hard, he'd thought at first that he'd gotten to her too late, and that she had been hit.

None of them had been shot, though. All three had escaped unscathed, with the exception of some minor bruises from falling to the ground. They were alive. And they were all well.

Ryder came back into the room. Isaac followed him, his expression grim. Ben knew that whatever they were going to say, he was definitely not going to like it. He wasn't going to like it at all. Ryder shut the door to give them some privacy and gestured to the table.

"Let's sit."

Ben waited for Sadie to straighten from her slump. Pulling out the chair next to her, he angled it so that he was close enough to touch her hand if he thought she needed his support. He was somewhat surprised when she reached out under the table and took his hand. Flicking his glance up to her profile, he was amazed. Her fingers trembled in his grasp, but her face was as calm and serene as if she were on her way to a church service, not preparing for news that had both Ryder and Isaac holding their mouths in grim lines.

His patience was thin as it took Ryder a bit to come to the point. Finally, the officer cleared his throat. "Here's the thing. We were not able to catch Mason Green as he fled the scene of the shooting. We have confirmed, both with your statements and with the camera from the stop light, that it was, in fact, Mr. Green driving the car."

"So he's still going to be coming after me."

He hated the dullness that had crept into Sadie's normally animated voice.

"Most likely." Ryder didn't look too happy with that thought. "The positive is that he still may not have an idea of where you are hiding. Yes, he saw you today. Which means he's been hanging around, and possibly has someone else helping him. And he's seen Ben, so he might recognize him. But he has not attacked at the Masts's home, nor have there been any reports of him around there. I have been keeping an eye out for him. So I think he hasn't realized that you're hiding there."

"He does know that I'm alive, though."

It was obvious that Ryder didn't know what they were referring to. It was then that Ben realized Ryder had no idea about what had happened on the trip to his family house. Sadie, apparently, came to the same conclusion. With a halting voice, she started telling about the storm and the accident on the interstate. Ben interjected a time or two when she left a detail out. When he heard about the explosion, Ryder's jaw dropped open.

"That's extreme," he managed to get out.

"*Jah*, it's extreme. It also gave us the benefit of time. He knows that we escaped, now, though I wonder why he was in town."

Again, it was too coincidental, and he didn't believe in coincidences.

"If I had to guess, I would say that he went back to search the wreckage of the cave, just to make you were in there. That would have taken him some time, as he would have needed to dig out the entrance. He might have given you a few days to run out of food or oxygen—"

Sadie's chair slid back and she jumped to her feet.

Ben leaned back, knowing she was going to start pacing the perimeter of the room. Which she did. Now that he knew for a fact who she was, he recalled that Sadie used to do the same thing as a child. It had made her mother crazy.

He shot forward in his seat. Her mother.

"Sadie." She stopped pacing and faced him.

"How did your mother die?"

Her shock showed in her eyes. "How—? She and my stepfather were killed in a fire."

"Was the fire in any way suspicious?"

She nodded. "The police believed it was started by some kids messing around who got careless."

"What if they weren't? What if Mason recognized your mom?"

She looked shaky at his questions. "But it was me—"

He shook his head. "You were a child. And you couldn't speak after the event. She, however, may have seen him around the farm before. He may not have wanted to take that chance."

"He has a point," Ryder mused. "Do you recall if you had seen him before the day he tried to kidnap you?"

Her face tightened, but he could see that she was trying to remember.

"I might have seen him before that, but I was only a child. I can remember nothing about him before the day he killed my father."

Ryder glanced at the clock in the corner of the room. "I think it's about time we got you home. I want to take a different car, in case Green's still out there."

On the ride back to his parents' house, Sadie was very quiet. It wasn't until after dinner, though, that they really had some time to talk.

"I don't know what to do," Sadie admitted. "Should I ask Ryder to hide me someplace else? I hate that I am putting your family at risk."

And he hated hearing her talk like that.

"Sadie, you're here. More than that, you have family here. Tomorrow, I want to take you to meet your grandparents."

"Grandparents," she echoed in a choked whisper. "I can't believe I have grandparents. I have no memory of them."

"They have never forgotten you or your mom."

"Why do you think she took me away?"

He pondered the question. "I think it was either to protect you because you saw your father's murderer, or it was because the pain of your father's death was overwhelming." He swallowed. "When my wife and daughter died, being here was excruciating. My parents wanted me to remarry, to give my son a mother. I couldn't do it."

"Is that why you left instead of moving into the *dawdi haus*?"

He nodded. "I'm a little ashamed now, but *jah*. That's why."

She placed a warm hand on his arm. He could feel the heat from her palm through his shirt. "Don't be ashamed, Ben. Everyone has to deal with pain. I'm sure they understood that you needed a break."

He smiled at her explanation. "I was gone for three years. That's a long break."

A chuckle broke from her. "You know what I mean."

"*Jah*, I know. *Denke* for caring."

For a moment, she didn't respond. He wondered if he had offended her. Then she responded so softly, he had trouble hearing her. "I care, Ben. I will always care."

True to his word, Ben took Sadie to meet her grand-parents the next day. The plan was that he would leave her there for a few hours so she could become reunited with her family. She knew that he had plans to help Isaac search the area and see if anyone had sighted Mason Green. Having her at a different location than she had been seemed like a good strategy.

Nathaniel had begged to go with them. The Bon-tragers, Esther explained, were a large family and had several children Nathaniel's age. Nathaniel was eager to meet them and play. Ben agreed. Until it was time for him to leave and Nathaniel said he wanted to stay and play with his new friends.

At first Ben hesitated. Sadie watched with amuse-ment as a very earnest child managed to wheedle his way through his father's objections until he was al-lowed to stay with the other children. No doubt he had decided that Nathaniel would be safer in a different en-vironment as well.

Sadie knew that Ben didn't want to leave, but she convinced him that she was well looked after. Besides her grandparents, she had several grown cousins pres-ent, as well, with their families. At first she was shy, not sure what they would expect of her or if she would be a disappointment to them, having grown up outside of the Amish life.

Instead, she found her grandparents to be two very warm and caring people. Her cousins seemed to wel-come her without hesitation, too. She was amazed at the sheer number of people there. It had always been her and Kurt. Now, it seemed, everywhere she looked there was another relative.

The moment that was really tense for her, however, was when the bishop stopped by to see her. What her mother had done in taking her from the Amish was grounds for being shunned or cast out. Not knowing what kind of reception to expect, Sadie was expecting the worst. When the bishop stood before her, she was sure she was going to get it. In her mind, she had done something selfish by coming to this district when she knew that someone was after her.

The bishop did not scold her, though. Instead, he asked her questions about her life with the *Englisch* and about her mother. He seemed to be genuinely sad to learn of her mother's death. She didn't add in her suspi-cion that her mother may have been murdered. Mostly because she didn't know yet if it was true.

"I remember your parents," he informed her. "I was

not bishop yet when you and your *mamm* left. Your father was a *gut* man. Hardworking and devoted to his family. Your mother was well known for baking the best pies in the district."

She remembered how her mother had loved to bake. A lump formed in her throat. As happy as she was to have her memories back, sometimes they were painful. Knowing that she had almost lost all knowledge of her mother made her ache with longing to see her again. She still didn't remember her father very well.

Lord, please let me get all my memories back.

She bit her lip. Was such a prayer selfish? On impulse, she asked the bishop. She almost regretted asking, though, at the surprised look that covered his face.

"You may pray to *Gott* about anything," he replied, to her relief. "*Gott* likes us to talk with Him."

When the bishop climbed back into his buggy to leave, she watched him go, feeling torn. She had so much to be thankful for. She had family she had lost. Family who truly cared about her. She had friends. Not only Isaac and Ben, but last night, Isaac had brought his wife, Lizzy, by to meet her.

Lizzy was like a ray of sunshine. She laughed and smiled, and joy just seemed to spill out of her. Sadie had been awkward at first, but the feeling had faded quickly in light of the other woman's enthusiasm.

Sadie thought they could become very close. If she were to stay. Part of her yearned to stay so much it was painful. She wanted to remain close to Esther and Abram, too.

But mostly she yearned to be able to stay with

Ben, whether he stayed here or returned home. She wanted to have the right to be the woman at his side as he raised his son. She thought that he would move back eventually and take over his father's business. Although he had not said so, she could read his attachment to this place in the way he talked about his family and in the pride he took in helping his father with his business.

Feeling pensive, she remained outside after the bishop left. Without thinking about where she was going, she began to walk along the driveway. Her thoughts returned to Ben.

His parents were right. It was time for Ben to start thinking about marrying again. Not that any woman could replace his Lydia. But she knew that it would be a good thing for him. And for Nathaniel.

She just didn't think she could be that woman. And she wanted to be. So very much.

Could she give up her life and return to the Amish? She grimaced. He had not asked her to. Had not even hinted that he wanted her to.

She had a life in the *Englisch* world. A job she enjoyed. A brother she cared about deeply. One who was still missing.

Had Kurt been able to find the information he needed to put his boss and Mason Green away? She felt that he had been making progress. And she knew that Ryder was looking very hard at the connection between Ethan Nettle and Mason Green.

It seemed too much of a coincidence that Ethan had hired Kurt after what happened with Sadie. And after both of her parents had died in such strange ways. Why had she never been attacked before now? Was it possible that the fact that she never spoke out had convinced them that she wouldn't tell? Or that she didn't know or understand what had happened to her real father?

Could he have hired Kurt to keep an eye on her?

She had been so young when her father had been killed. So young, that she knew she didn't look the same as she had before. And with her not being Amish anymore, could Ethan have questioned whether or not she was the girl who got away, the girl who had seen Mason Green's face?

Maybe it was a test for her brother. Or maybe it was a test for her, to see if she had remembered.

As she mused, she absently walked around to the front of the house and paced on the driveway. Ice slid down her spine. Her entire life seemed like a setup. There were just too many things that led back to that fateful day when Mason Green had attempted to steal her away so many years ago.

"Sadie? Sadie, is that you?"

She turned at the masculine voice. Frowning slightly, she watched as a young man hurried over to her. Through a short beard, a wide smile stretched across his friendly face. He wasn't handsome, but she could see a definite charm about him. He wore a flannel shirt and blue jeans, and a dark brown leather jacket.

Not Amish. As he came closer, she felt no inkling that she had ever seen him before. Had she completely forgotten parts of her adult life, too? She had thought all of those memories had returned, but she must have been mistaken.

The young man, who was about her age, halted a few feet from her. A sense of unease swept over her. She didn't know him. And his smile was wide, but his eyes…

There was something cold in his eyes. And why would she know an *Englischer* out here, when she hadn't been in this area for so many years?

"I'm sorry. I don't have time to talk right now." She tried to excuse herself, backing away from him.

He took a step closer to her, again closing the gap between them. His smile tightened, although it remained on his face. It gained a chilling quality that made her cringe on the inside.

"What's the rush? Certainly you have time to catch up with an old friend?" His voice was pleasant. Teasing, even.

She was now certain that this man was not a friend. She didn't think she had ever seen him before. He was not here to catch up with her, or for any other benign purpose.

Inside, her instincts were telling her to flee. He was so close to her, she could smell the mint of his breath. Normally a pleasing aroma, it made her stomach turn. She was farther away from her grandparents' house than she had thought. If she turned and ran, she might make it. But she doubted it.

As if he sensed her thoughts, his hand shot out and grabbed her. His leather jacket gaped open and she swallowed. He was wearing a gun under his jacket, confirming her suspicions that he was here for reasons that had nothing to do with friendship.

He followed her gaze. His smile morphed into a steely grin. "Ah, yes. You have found out my little secret. It helps to encourage those who are less than willing to hear me out."

She backed up another step. "I don't know you. I need to go back." She tugged at her arm. He held on. His grip tightened painfully.

"I don't think so, Sadie. You have made things very difficult for my father. You and that brother of yours."

Kurt. He was talking about Kurt. Had Kurt been found by the criminals? Her heartbeat was thudding in her ears.

"He has gone into hiding, but maybe if his little sister is in need, he'll come out to help her."

So they didn't have Kurt yet. That was good. How was she going to get away? She glanced around, desperate to find a weapon of some kind. A way to distract him.

"Oh, no. You are not getting away this time. My father has wasted so much time trusting Mason Green to haul you in, but he hasn't. You're too slippery. But you're not smarter than I am. I'm going to be the one to get you. Then my father will see that he should let me in for a bigger part of the business."

With a sudden twist, she wrenched out of his grip and turned to run. He caught up with her before she'd taken four steps. One hand grabbed her shoulder, the other latched on to her *kapp*. And her hair. Pain had tears stinging her eyes as he pulled her back. Forcing her to face him again, he removed the hand on her *kapp*. The garment fell to the ground.

"That wasn't smart, Sadie. I don't have much patience."

While he was talking, he began to drag her away from her family's house. She opened her mouth, drawing breath to scream.

"You scream and you'll be dead before anyone gets to you. I have people watching the Amish people you're staying with. That little boy is adorable."

His insinuation made her breath stick in her throat, nearly choking her. He'd hurt Nathaniel, or worse. She had no choice. She must protect those she loved at all costs. She stopped struggling. He chuckled and continued to drag her down the block.

"That's right. I knew you were smart."

"Sadie! Let her go!" Nathaniel charged down the street and launched himself at the man. With a growl, the man swatted him away.

"Get in the car, Sadie, and I won't take him with us."

"Stay there, Nathaniel," she told the child, terrified he wouldn't listen. She saw his tear-damp face staring at her, but he didn't move. She was amazed that he was being allowed to go free. He was a potential witness.

They had arrived at a small sedan. Knowing she couldn't let her captor harm Nathaniel, she obediently climbed into the back seat and lay on the floorboards. He threw some blankets over her, covering her up. "You make any dumb move, and the kid will suffer."

She was suffocating under the blankets. Sweat began to pool on her neck. Her forehead grew damp. Something heavy was placed on top of the blankets, holding her in place.

Fear drew her down. She felt more than heard the car start, and the motion as it started moving made her want to vomit.

She was out of time.

FOURTEEN

Sadie lost track of how much time had passed or how many turns they had taken. Several times she lost consciousness due to a combination of the heat and the panic that she was swimming in. Would she ever see Ben and Nathaniel again? Her brother?

So many things she regretted not saying, now that it was too late.

Sadie knew she was going to die. But at least her brother and the others were safe. She was very grateful that he had let Nathaniel go. Hopefully Kurt would get the evidence to stop these men before they destroyed too many other lives.

It hurt, the fear and the anxiety that crawled through her. Silent tears slid down her face.

After what could've been half an hour or two hours, the car came to a final stop. She felt the engine turn off. A few seconds later, the front door of the vehicle slammed. When she heard the vibration, she braced herself, knowing that he would open the door and pull her out to meet whatever fate awaited her.

Ethan Nettle had a son. On some level she had been aware of this. She tried to think if she could remember hearing his name before. She couldn't.

As she had feared, moments later the weights were lifted from her and the blankets came off. Opening her eyes, she once again came face-to-face with her captor. The friendly smile was gone, replaced with terrifying determination. His long arms reached out and he dragged her to her feet. She stumbled slightly as he yanked her out of the car. Her legs were unsteady from being kept in such an uncomfortable position. She fell awkwardly against him. He pushed her away and slapped her face. Her eyes watered in response to the pain on her cheek.

"Come on. Don't make any trouble," he warned her and then proceeded to half drag, half carry her into a building that seemed familiar. He pulled her down a flight of stairs. With some horror, she realized that she was in the basement of the newspaper office where her brother worked.

Forcing her to sit on a chair in the corner, he securely tied her hands and her feet, making her escape impossible. She could barely move, the bonds were so tight. She watched as he reached up and ripped off his beard. She hadn't realized it was a fake.

"That's better. I don't know how anyone can stand those things. I really should have grabbed the kid," he mused, making her blood boil. "It would have been too much trouble, though. It's not like he can identify me." Smirking, he pointed to his now clean-shaven face. Then he pulled out his phone and looked at it. The satisfied smile that crossed his lips was one of the scariest things she had ever seen. "Good. All you have to do now is wait. I have called my father. He's on his way. I'm sure he's bringing that idiot Green with him, but at least he'll know that I managed to do in one attempt what Green couldn't." He snickered. It wasn't an attractive sound. "He couldn't even get you out of the way with explosives."

A sound near the door distracted him. As he peered into the shadows, a figure shot forward and attacked. She watched as the two men wrestled.

Kurt.

Her foolish brother was fighting with the man who had kidnapped her. Fear and hope trembled inside her. And she was helpless to do more than watch. Suddenly, a third person was in the room.

Mason Green. He took one look at the scene before him and laughed before he hefted something in the air and brought it down on Kurt's head. Kurt fell to the ground, and Green let the wrench he was holding drop from his hands.

"So, you can be useful," Ethan's son sneered.

"Can it, Vincent. You almost got taken down. What would your father have said then?"

The amount of antagonism between the two men was frightening. Both of them, it seemed, would do anything for the approval of Ethan Nettle. The man she had thought was her brother's friend was the leader of men such as these. Kurt groaned from the floor. Her shoulders slumped. She hadn't allowed herself to imagine him dead, but the realization that he wasn't sang through her blood.

At least, he wasn't dead yet. They were in a horrible predicament. One she wasn't sure she had a way out of.

Ben would turn it over to God. Keeping her eyes on the two men in front of her, she said a quick prayer in her mind. She asked God to watch over them and help them escape. But if they couldn't escape, she asked Him to watch over Ben, Nathaniel and Isaac. And their families.

"Let's tie him up before he comes completely to his senses," Ethan's son ordered.

"Listen, you, you're not in charge here." Green bristled with anger.

"Really? Because it kind of seems that I am. Now, are we going to tie this dude up, or do you want to explain to my dad why he was roaming free when he arrives?"

She noticed that Vincent stressed the words *my dad.* He was letting the other man know that he was flesh and blood and the other man was merely hired help. Mason Green's complexion changed to a mottled red, his eyes hot with his anger. But he did as Vincent Nettle had ordered.

Within minutes, Kurt was tied up on the floor near her chair. He wasn't completely conscious yet, but she knew it was just a matter of time.

The thump of heavy footsteps coming down the stairs brought everyone's attention to the door. Ethan Nettle appeared and took in the scene. His sharp business suit and carefully trimmed hair was so urbane and the epitome of a charming businessman, Sadie's gut lurched. He used his power, and his job, to enable him to do heinous acts. He needed to be stopped. Only she was in no position to stop him.

His eyes landed on her, and she cringed. How had she not noticed how cruel his gaze could be?

"Vincent, you did well, son. Do you see, Mason? This is how it's done. Both of the Standings, literally at my feet."

Mason Green fumed, his mouth a hard slash across his face as he glared at his competition. Vincent smirked. Then he rubbed salt in the wound.

"It wasn't hard, Dad. All I needed to do to get her was to make sure she knew that the kid we saw her with would be in danger if she didn't cooperate."

She didn't like the gleam that entered Ethan's eyes as he stared at her. "Maybe he will anyway. As an example."

She struggled with her restraints, knowing it was useless, but fueled with the urgent need to protect Nathaniel from these vicious men.

All three of them laughed.

Ethan stepped closer to her. "You are well and truly caught, my dear." He turned his contemptuous gaze to Kurt, whose eyes were now open and watching. "All you had to do was keep out of my business. I was almost convinced that your sister knew nothing. She would have been safe, because too many accidents draw too much attention. But you had to dig. I knew you had to die," he said, turning back to Sadie, "when it looked like you recognized the picture of Mason that night I ate dinner at your house." He jerked his thumb at the man behind him.

"Did you kill my mother and stepfather?"

The words left her mouth before she even knew she was going to say them. He grinned, a nasty expression that curdled her blood. Kurt's head jerked up. He had never suspected that their parents' deaths was anything but an accident.

"She was a loose end I couldn't afford. She had seen Mason one day, and I knew the risk was too great. Don't worry. They didn't suffer. Much."

She shuddered, and he laughed.

Apparently bored with the conversation, Ethan Nettle turned to his son. "We need to get ready. After these two are taken care of, things will be too hot for us around here. We need to be prepared."

Vincent nodded and started up the stairs. Ethan watched his son leave the room, then he turned back to Mason Green.

Green stood straighter. "You have disappointed me several times now, Mason. I hope this is not a trend that continues."

"No boss. I know what to do."

"Good." Satisfaction settled on Ethan's face. He was a handsome man, but at the moment, he was ugly, marred by the evil that lurked in his heart. "I'll leave you to finish this mess. I don't have to tell you that I am counting on you."

After receiving his employee's nod, Ethan turned on his heel and headed out, following his son up the stairs without a backward glance at the two people he'd just condemned to death.

Sadie braced herself as Mason turned to them. "Well. I see we are to meet one last time, little girl. Too bad only one of us will make it out of here alive."

Ben returned with his buggy to collect Sadie and Nathaniel at the appointed time. He smiled to himself as he recalled her excitement when he'd introduced her to her grandparents. She had been apprehensive, too, but he knew it would be well. The Bontragers had suffered with the death of their son and the disappearance of his widow and child.

They didn't blame Hannah for leaving. The love for a child and the urge to protect her was a powerful force. He wondered what he would have done if something had threatened Nathaniel. He didn't even want to go there.

He stopped his buggy halfway up the driveway and descended. He asked one of the women on the porch to point him to where Sadie was.

"She went for a walk with the bishop. He left to go attend to other duties. She never came back."

"I saw her walking down the driveway. She might have gone for a walk," one of her many cousins reported.

Thanking them brusquely, he hurried in the direction the girl had indicated. He felt a sense of urgency. Something was wrong. Sadie was not one to concern others by wandering off. She had more sense than that. No one here understood the danger as he did. Why had she walked away from the house?

Footsteps ran up behind him. "*Dat!* He has her. The bad man has her!"

His son's words were enough to drop him to his knees. He caught Nathaniel as the child flew into his arms, slamming into his father hard enough to rock him back on his heels. The boy was sobbing so fiercely he was struggling to breathe.

"Settle down, Nathaniel. You have to tell me what happened. Then we can help Sadie. Can you tell me what happened?" he asked when his son seemed to be calmer.

The boy's lips trembled. "A man was dragging her down the street. She was fighting him, *Dat*. She looked scared. I ran after them and tried to stop the bad man from taking her."

His heart was in his throat. His brave little boy had tried to take on a killer to protect Sadie. He'd come so close to having them both taken. He looked down, and paled. Nathaniel had a white prayer *kapp* in his hands. Sadie's *kapp*.

He was afraid to speak again.

"He hit me and I fell. Then he told Sadie he'd let me go if she stopped fighting. She told me to stay. He made her get into his car and made her lie on the floor."

"How long ago was this?"

Nathaniel shrugged, his face miserable. "I don't know. She told me to stay, so I stayed. I sat there until I saw you come, then I wanted to tell you what had happened."

Ben took a deep breath. He needed to find her. *Gott, help me.*

"Nathaniel, I need you to go and stay inside the *haus* with the Bontragers. I need to find Sadie, and it will be easier if I know you are safe."

The little boy threw his arms around his father and squeezed him tight. Ben's eyes closed as emotions swamped him. "Bring her home, *Dat.*"

Home. "I will, son. If it's possible, I will."

He knew better than to promise something like that, but he couldn't stop himself.

Nathaniel nodded, then ran up the drive and into the house. Now that he knew Nathaniel was safe, Ben could work on finding Sadie and bringing her back.

Running to his buggy, he climbed up and turned around in record time. Every second to Isaac's house seemed to be a second lost. Isaac was a former police officer. Ben hoped he would get in touch with Ryder and they would find her.

Please Gott, *let us find her before it's too late.*

He had no doubt that Mason Green had found her. And knowing the history she had with that man, it wasn't hard to imagine what he would do with her. Sweat broke out on Ben's forehead.

He had the fear that they would find her body. He blocked those thoughts from his mind. Sadie would be all right. She had to be. And when he found her, he would forget his pride and all his nonsense about not interfering with her choice and would ask her to rejoin the church and be his bride. Even if she said no, he could no longer pretend that his feelings for her would fade once she left.

Isaac and Lizzy both waved as he pulled into their

driveway. One look at his face, though, and Isaac was all business. His friend and his wife were waiting for him the second he pulled on the reins to command the horse to halt.

"He has her," Ben gasped. Lizzy paled. Isaac didn't hesitate.

"There's a phone in the barn," he called out, racing toward it.

Ben was right behind him. Isaac placed the call to Ryder, then he followed Ben back to the buggy. "We need to question the people on the street, see if they have anything to add. Maybe one of them saw something."

It seemed to take forever to get back to where Sadie had disappeared. They questioned the neighbors at each house. The fourth was the home of a young *Englisch* couple. The twenty something husband answered the door, looking startled to have a couple of Amish men on his porch.

"Can I help you?"

"Yes," Isaac responded. "Probably around an hour ago, a young Amish woman was abducted from the Bontrager farm four houses down. A young boy saw her being dragged into a car. Did you happen to see anything suspicious around that time?"

The young man removed his ball cap and scratched his head. "I'm sorry to hear about the woman. A car did come and stop in front of the Bontrager house. I noticed it sitting there when I went out to go to the store. I didn't see who was driving it, but I do recall thinking that it was weird to see a car parked in front of the house."

Ben's heart sped up. Hopefully this man would be able to provide some information that would help them.

Isaac continued to ask him questions. The man hadn't seen the driver, but he definitely got a good look at the car. He was able to provide them with the make and model of the sedan, along with the color and the college sticker in the back window.

"Thanks. This might help us locate her," Isaac told the man.

Ten minutes later, they were joined by Ryder. From where he stood, Ben could see Lily patiently sitting in the front seat.

Succinctly, they told him all they had learned. Within minutes, he had called in the description of the car in what he called a BOLO or *be on the lookout*.

"Once we get a hit, we will head in that direction. I brought Lily along. I know you said Sadie was taken by car. But once she is out of the car, Lily can help. She might be able to track Sadie's scent. If you have anything of Sadie's with you, that is."

Ben started to shake his head, then stopped. Sadie's *kapp*. He handed it over to Ryder, his hands shaking slightly.

Ryder met his eyes. "We'll do our best to find her, Ben. I promise you that I will use whatever I can to find her."

Ben nodded, his throat closed.

Isaac placed his hand on Ben's shoulder briefly in solidarity. The hand slipped off when Ryder's radio started beeping before a feminine voice broke through. Ryder straightened and answered the call. Ben clenched and unclenched his hands, trying to understand the jargon that was passing back and forth between the sergeant and the dispatcher.

"We have a sighting." Ryder turned and strode back to his car. "Let's go. Someone saw the car in the downtown area ten minutes ago."

Ben and Isaac ran after Ryder. Both of them climbed into the back seat.

"I'm not going to use my siren. I don't want to give Green a heads-up that he's been found." He pulled the car out onto the road. When they hit the downtown area, Ben swallowed his disappointment as they hit some minor traffic. Every second wasted was a second longer that Sadie was in the hands of evil men.

"You should hit the lights, even if you're not going to use the siren," Isaac advised tensely. Ben realized that Isaac was affected by the kidnapping of their childhood friend, too.

"Yep." Ryder flicked a switch, and Ben could see the reflection of the flashing lights on the windshields of the cars they passed. The vehicles ahead of them moved to the side, allowing the cruiser to speed up the road uninhibited.

Gib nicht auf, Sadie. Ben whispered the words in his mind, silently pleading with her not to give up. *We're coming.*

He could only pray they'd be in time.

FIFTEEN

Ryder turned the corner so sharply that Ben set a hand down on the seat to balance himself. He didn't complain. Anything that Ryder did in pursuit of Sadie was fine with him. When the police officer pulled to a stop behind the car that fit the description of the vehicle the young man had described, he felt his hopes rise.

Three men climbed from the car. Ben didn't recognize the area. Ryder jogged to the other side of the cruiser and let Lily out. He snapped a leash on her harness and then he held Sadie's *kapp* to her nose. Lily sniffed the *kapp*, quivering.

When he told her to search in German, Ben blinked. He hadn't expected that the dog would have been trained in such a familiar language.

"It made sense to teach her in a language I could remember," Isaac murmured, his eyes focused on his former colleague and the canine cop.

Lily put her muzzle to the ground and then shot off to the back door of the building.

Where were they? Frowning, Ben looked around.

Isaac caught his breath beside him. "The newspaper's office is in this building. We need to be careful."

Ryder nodded. "We don't have a warrant, but I think we have a strong case for not waiting for one." He thumbed the radio on his shoulder. When it was answered, he gave their location and the situation. "The situation is grave. I can't wait to enter the building, but I am requesting backup as soon as possible."

"Backup will be there in under ten."

Ten minutes. They couldn't wait. Not for other officers, not for a warrant. Ben didn't care about the *Englisch* laws. He was going in, whether they were allowed to or not. Sadie's life was in the balance, and that mattered more than any law.

"Let's take this slowly," Ryder warned. "I don't want to frighten him. It might go bad for Sadie."

Isaac nodded and Ben understood what he was saying. If they made Mason Green aware of their presence, he might hurt Sadie, or worse, and try to get away again. He was all for going careful if it would protect her.

Lord, please keep her safe. Help us to catch this man and keep him from preying on other women and children.

He thought of how Nathaniel said that the man who took Sadie had threatened to take him along, as well. If that had happened, he might have lost both of those he loved most without any idea of where they should start searching for them. He wasn't sure how he would have gotten through that, although he knew *Gott* would be there to help him.

"Okay, let's go around the side of the building,"

Ryder whispered, breaking into his bleak thoughts. "There's another entrance there. It might help us sneak up on them."

Ryder went first with Lily. The other two men followed, trying to keep the noise down. Together, they went around to the side. Ryder and Isaac opened the door slowly. A very slight creak sounded from the heavy door, but hopefully it was masked by the other noises around them. As soon as they entered, Lily's nose was on the ground again as she continued to search for her target. The next five minutes felt like an hour as they crept after the canine. At last, they could hear the low rumble of masculine voices. One voice. Two voices. Ben's eyebrow raised. He thought he recognized Kurt's voice. Even though he couldn't understand what his friend was saying, he thought he could detect the fear and strain in his voice.

He glanced at Isaac and Ryder. Both were looking grim.

Suddenly, Kurt shouted out. A second later, Ben heard a scream that made his blood turn to ice in his veins. Sadie. He was done waiting. He took off in the direction of the scream, followed closely by Isaac and Ryder. He twisted around a corner, his blood pounding in his ears.

More shouts by Kurt kept him moving in the direction of the voices. They led him to a staircase. He stomped rapidly down the stairs, not even caring anymore that he was making enough noise to alert everyone in the building to his presence.

Ryder shoved past him, gun out.

"Police! Drop your weapon!" Ryder shouted, pointing his gun at someone still out of Ben's sight. A second later, Ben and Isaac reached the bottom of the steps together and took in the room at a glance.

Kurt was lying on his side, tied up. He must have fallen over or been pushed. He was awake and had some slight facial bruising.

Directly in front of them, Mason Green was holding on to a struggling Sadie. Ben kept his eyes focused on Mason with difficulty. If he looked at her, he was afraid that the strength of his emotions, one of which was a hot rage that was constricting his chest, would take over his common sense.

She was alive. He needed to focus on that and not let himself be sidetracked by other things. Right now, getting her out of this alive and without further harm was his priority.

Sirens were heard directly outside the building.

"Drop the gun, Green. There's no way you can get away with hurting Miss Standings or Mr. Standings. You're going to be arrested, and any additional violence will only hurt your chances when you go to trial."

Mason Green laughed harshly. Then he sneered. "I'm not the one you should be worried about. The Nettles are long gone. You'll never find them."

Ryder narrowed his eyes. "I wouldn't count on that."

Ben held himself still to keep from drawing attention. He caught Sadie's eye, trying to communicate his love and his promise to free her. She didn't look away. When he looked back at Mason Green for a moment, he saw when the man lost all hope and only wanted his vengeance.

Mason's eyes twitched to where he was holding Sadie. Ben knew he was planning on shooting her.

The moment he brought the gun closer and his finger tightened on the trigger, Sadie yelled out, her voice vibrating with fury, and kicked, hard. Mason screamed in pain as the heel of her boot slammed into his shin. She jerked from his loosened hold. Ben leaped forward, catching Sadie and dropping to the floor with her in his arms. Kurt yelled. A gunshot went wild, hitting the wall.

Ryder attacked, rushing at Mason and taking him down. Within seconds, the angry man was struggling and shouting, even as Ryder rolled him over and cuffed him while yelling his rights at full voice.

When the man was subdued, Isaac assisted Ryder in pulling him to his feet. He had to dodge out of the way to avoid being kicked. Ben turned away from Mason, his full attention on the young woman who held his heart. Without thinking about it, he kissed her gently on the forehead. Then on the cheek.

He wanted to kiss her lips, desperately. But he held himself back. Instead, he stood and held out his hand. She put hers in his, and he gently tugged her to her feet. Carefully, he scrutinized her, looking for any outward signs of injury. She had a couple of scratches and a bruise on the right side of her face. Other than that, she appeared unharmed. He sighed in relief.

All the fears he'd kept inside for the past hour caught up with him. He could feel himself starting to shake. He slammed his eyes closed and clenched his fists, doing his best to hold himself together. Nothing worked.

"Ben."

He opened his eyes and stared into the eyes of the woman he had risked death to save. She was the most beautiful thing he'd ever seen.

"You came," she choked out. "I can't believe you found me."

"I promised I would protect you. I meant it. With my whole being."

He was unprepared for the suddenness with which she flung her arms around him and snuggled into his shoulder. He adapted well, though, and his own arms closed around her. He stood there, silently praising *Gott* for protecting her and letting him hold her in his arms.

Sadie wanted nothing more than to stay nestled deep in Ben's strong embrace. But she knew she couldn't. She had to move away from him. Instinctively, her arms tightened in protest. She inhaled his clean, comforting scent.

Enough. This was already hard. She needed to stop torturing them both.

Bracing herself, she backed out of his grasp. He released her, and his arms fell to his sides. She saw his fingers twitch, as if they wanted to reach out and hold her again. They didn't, though.

She was glad, she told herself, even as she wrestled with the regret.

"I thought we were too late," he whispered.

It was then that she noticed Isaac helping Kurt to his

feet while Ryder took a handcuffed Mason Green out to his cruiser. The killer impaled her with a deadly glare and sneered as he was paraded past her. "Don't get too complacent, little girl. Ethan will finish the job. Don't you doubt that."

It wasn't over, even though they had caught Mason Green.

Horrified, she swiveled her head and looked at Ben. The Amish man's mouth was a tight line, and his eyes were hard as he watched the criminal being put in the back of the police car.

"Ben?"

She had to call his name a second time before he stopped glaring after Mason Green and turned his attention back to her. There was no mistaking the concern in those deep eyes. She had grown familiar with his moods.

"They're still going to be after me."

Please say I'm wrong. Please.

He didn't. Instead, his face grew grim as he slowly nodded. "*Jah*. We already knew that Mason Green was working with Ethan Nettle."

"It's not just Ethan. His son Vincent is working with him." She saw the surprise in his eyes. "I so hoped it was over." She couldn't control her glance in the direction that Ryder had taken Mason. She knew that by now, the villain was safe inside the police cruiser. She couldn't see Mason through the walls, but she felt as though his eyes were boring holes in her, even from a distance. "Ethan and his son were here. Vincent was the man that kidnapped me. They were already packed and

ready to disappear. After Ethan scolded Mason for fail-
ing too many times. In order to make up for past mis-
takes, Mason's job was to get rid of Kurt and myself."

Ben paled at her words.

Would she never be safe?

"You could come back—"

"No. I'm sorry, Ben. I will not put you or your family
in danger again."

He sighed. "They are your people, too, Sadie. You
have family there. Family that loves you." He paused,
his gaze searching her face. "You could join the church.
I'm sure you could find a *mann*. Maybe even one who
is a lonely widower, who would open his heart and his
home to you."

She couldn't breathe. Ben, the man she had being
trying so hard to deny her growing feelings for, was
all but telling her he loved her and wished for her to be
his wife. The mother of his children.

For the space of three heartbeats, she almost agreed,
her heart filling with joy at this gift. Then reality
crashed in, shattering the dreams. She couldn't do it.
Couldn't put them in danger. The Amish were peaceful people. If killers came for her family, Ben would
not pick up a gun to protect himself. He would protect
his family, but for himself he would accept death rather
than participate in violence. That would destroy her.

She swallowed the pain that started to fill her heart
and stepped back from him, deliberately increasing the
distance. His face paled, telling her he understood her
move.

"I am not going back to the Amish district, Ben. I

will not continue to put you and Nathaniel, or my family and friends in danger. It wouldn't be fair."

"You belong with us," he insisted, his voice rough with hurt.

Oh, no. Tears stung her eyes. She wanted to give in and tell him she'd go anywhere he was. But it would never work. And she didn't know if she could live a life under the fear and pressure.

"Nee." The Amish word slipped out. "I do not belong anywhere. I am not *Englisch*, not anymore, nor am I Amish. I won't be responsible for putting anyone in danger. Not again."

Ryder came to where they stood. His serious eyes bounced between them. Had he heard what they had been talking about? His words confirmed that he had.

"If you won't return to the Amish with Ben, you should still go into hiding. Ethan Nettle and his son are both gone. It won't be safe for you to return to your home. I will have to put a security detail on Kurt, too."

Her brother. Maybe she'd be able to be placed with him. Then she wouldn't be alone.

"I can't go into a safe house," Kurt stated in a voice tinged with steel, coming over to their group, dashing her hopes. "Not now that I know Ethan is a part of this."

"Kurt," she started, then paused, unsure what to say.

"My boss is Mason Green's contact," Kurt growled. "I can't believe I never suspected it."

"It's because of me," she whispered. Kurt glanced at her, his face alert. "Oh, Kurt, I had blocked the memories, but Mason Green had murdered my real father, years ago. My mother and I left our home so she could protect me. When Ethan was at our house, I saw a photo of Mason, and my reaction told Ethan that I had recognized it, although I still didn't recall completely who he was."

Kurt shook his head. "He's been playing me the whole time. My guess is in his mind, I was expendable. Maybe he's been using me to figure out what you knew. How much of a threat you were. Once he knew you were remembering, I'm sure he was pretty desperate to get you out of the picture. I can't let them get away with that."

"What do you plan to do?" Ben asked, subdued.

She winced. He was still hurt by her rejection, but she knew she'd made the right choice.

"I'm a reporter," Kurt responded. "I'm going to do my job and expose the truth."

Ryder walked over to Sadie. "I can put you in a safe place. If you are sure this is what you want. I can arrange for a temporary placement for you until we find Nettle and his son. Nettle has a very well-known face. In order to truly hide, he'll have to be in disguise. There's no telling how long this could take."

Sadie bit her lip. She knew that they were all thinking the same thing. What if they never found Nettle or his son? She'd be in hiding for the rest of her life. Never to see Kurt again. Separated from her newly discovered grandparents…and from the man she—

No. That was done. It had to be. There was nothing for her in that relationship.

Turning to Ryder, she tightened her jaw. "That's what I want."

He nodded. Ben's eyes glistened, but he didn't argue. Her heart shattered as she watched him straighten his shoulders and walk away.

Taking her heart with him.

SIXTEEN

Sadie opened the door to find Ryder standing on the other side. In the four months since she'd left Ben and gone into hiding, she and the officer had become friends. He was her one connection to Ben and to her brother. The one thing that kept her from going out of her mind as she waited to hear that she could finally go home and begin to live her life again were his visits, where he would tell her how the case was proceeding.

"Ryder. I wasn't expecting you today." She opened the door wider and stepped back, allowing him to enter the apartment she was staying in. She really didn't like the apartment. Oh, there was nothing wrong with it. It was clean, and although it was small, it had everything she needed.

It just wasn't home.

She was distracted momentarily when she realized that when she thought of home, the image that filled her mind wasn't the house she shared with her brother. No, when she thought of home, she thought of Ben and Nathaniel. She had been thinking about them a lot. She couldn't seem to go through an hour without something reminding her of the two of them.

She needed to wrap her mind around the fact that she was not a part of their lives. Not anymore. Ben was an attractive, intelligent man. One who had led her back to God. She would always be grateful to him. But despite the fact that her roots were in the Amish world, she was part of the *Englisch* world now.

Ryder called her name. Shaking herself from the depths of her reverie, she blinked at him, feeling herself flush at being caught daydreaming.

"Sadie, I have some news for you."

She scoured his face with her gaze. News could be a good thing or it could be very, very bad. She had to be ready for anything. That meant fortification. Which meant coffee.

"Come into the kitchen. I just made coffee."

He followed her into the small kitchen area, just large enough to accommodate a small square table butted up against the wall and two wooden chairs. It was sparse, but she found she was comfortable in the simplicity. She would have liked more room so she could bake easily, but she never complained.

Grabbing two mugs from the rack on the counter, she poured out the hot, strong coffee, then put the cream and sugar on the table. She didn't use it, although she had before she knew Ben, but she knew her friend liked to doctor his coffee.

Ben. Why couldn't she get through five minutes without thinking about the man?

"I hope you are bringing me good news." Sitting

across from Ryder, she held her mug in both hands, enjoying the warmth. It was bitterly cold outside, with a fresh layer of glittering snow on the ground. There was a lot to be said for staying inside on days like this.

"I think I have good news." Ryder took a sip and set his mug back on the table. He leaned forward. "We found Ethan and Vincent Nettle."

Her breath caught in her throat. Almost afraid to speak, she whispered, "Is it over?"

"Almost. Mason Green is set to go to trial in three weeks. With his partners put away, there is no one out there to go after you."

"What about the man who was sent to prison for killing my father?"

He grimaced. "Unfortunately, we can't give the man those sixteen years back. He was a teenager then. He has spent his entire young adulthood in prison. He's bitter, and of course there will always be people who will refuse to believe that he didn't do anything wrong. But he's a free man. His record has been expunged, so he won't have the limitations an ex-con might face. It's up to him to make a good life for himself."

She'd be bitter, too, if the system had failed her that badly. Would he be able to come to terms with the loss of sixteen years and move on? It would be a shame if he allowed what had happened to ruin the remainder of his years.

She stilled.

"Sadie? Are you okay? You've gone awful pale."

She heard Ryder's voice as if it were coming through a tunnel.

"I want to go back," she said out loud. She felt as though God had given her a sudden clarity. She had hoped Jeffrey wouldn't allow his past to dictate his future, but wasn't she doing the same thing? She had decided that, because of the actions of others, she had to make a life in the *Englisch* world, even if it wasn't a life that she felt she belonged in anymore.

"Back? Yes, that's what I'm trying to tell you. You can come out of hiding and you can go back. I can't promise your job is still there, but I'm sure you can find another—"

"No, no. You don't understand." She stood and moved to the window. "I can go all the way back. Back home. Back to my family."

Back to Ben and Nathaniel.

Fear and trepidation rose up and made it hard to speak. What if Ben didn't want her back? She'd disrupted his life while she was there.

The kiss they'd shared might be the only one she'd ever receive from him, but she needed to know if they could have a future.

There could be nothing between them if she stayed *Englisch*.

"You want to go to Ben." It wasn't a question. Ryder shoved his chair back and stretched his long legs in front of him.

"Is that wrong?" She winced at the defensiveness in her tone.

He shook his head, his face growing thoughtful. "No, not wrong. But I'm just thinking. When Isaac knew he was in love with Lizzy—"

Her face warmed.

"He knew he couldn't go to her without being a part of the Amish community he'd left all those years before."

"Yeah, I can understand that. She was a baptized member of the Amish church. That makes total sense."

"Right. But he couldn't go to her right away."

No. No. No. She'd already waited so long.

"But—"

"Sadie." She folded her arms and listened, not liking where this conversation was going. He continued. "I'm not telling you what to do. I'm just telling you, as a friend, what another friend went through to find his way back to his girl. He said that he had to be sure that the Amish life was what he wanted for all time. And that he couldn't approach her until he was one hundred percent sure."

She sighed. He was right.

And then there was Kurt. She couldn't abandon her brother without warning. He'd be so hurt if she got out of hiding and immediately left. She needed to contact the bishop, privately, and let him know she wished to come home. And then she needed to get the life she was leaving in order. And only then could she go back.

"You're right. I can't go back to being Amish because of Ben. Although he is a major incentive. I have to be willing to live that life even if he and I don't become a couple."

"Exactly."

A new excitement was building inside her. Did she have a future with Ben and Nathaniel? She loved him; she could admit it to herself. And she wanted to be the one he chose to be the mother Nathaniel needed. In her mind, she could envision herself holding an infant, Ben and Nathaniel beside her. She flushed. And smiled to herself at the thought of making a family with the man she'd been ready to give up for good.

"I have so much to do."

"I'll give you a hand."

Ryder assisted her as she packed up her meager belongings. It only took a couple of hours. When they had packed the last box, he pulled out his phone.

"I have a truck coming by to get your things."

She didn't question it until she saw the familiar pickup truck pull into the driveway. With a squeal, she dashed outside without her coat and threw herself at her brother the second he stepped down from the vehicle, never feeling the cold. Kurt's arms closed around her tightly. She could feel them tremble slightly and knew that he was as emotional as she at their reunion.

"Good to see you, sis," he muttered in a rough voice.

"I am so happy you're here." She hugged him again. She mentally thanked God for blessing her with the return of her memories so that she could appreciate what a wonderful man her brother was. She wouldn't lose her connection with him if she returned to the Amish world, she knew that, but it was bittersweet being reunited with him, knowing she'd be leaving again.

But she needed to find the place God had planned for her.

"Hey, buddy, I thought you might want to see this." Isaac's words cut through the fog that had encompassed Ben's brain since Sadie left him. Or, more precisely, since she'd gone into hiding. It seemed like years ago, yet it had only been five months. Setting his tools aside, he looked up to see Isaac standing in the door to his shop, a newspaper in his hands.

He shrugged and stood back from the table, stretching to work out the ache in his back. It was time for him to take a break, anyhow.

"*Buddy?* That's very *Englisch* of you."

Isaac grinned. "What can I say? I lived in that world for seven years. I picked up some things."

Ben huffed out a chuckle. "What do I need to see?"

"Oh, yeah." Isaac held out the paper. Ben took it, still mystified. "Here."

Following the line of his friend's finger to where he pointed, Ben saw the article and noticed Kurt's name on the byline. "Page one? Kurt's moving up."

"Yeah, yeah. Read the story."

Ben sat down and read. After the third paragraph, he needed to sit as the meaning of what he was reading started to sink in. Mason Green was dead. The man who had murdered Sadie's father and let another man take the fall had been killed in prison awaiting trial. The police had his partners in custody, all profits and assets had been seized and the evidence of their involvement in the drug trade and practice of selling children had been collected and documented. There was enough to put them away for the rest of their lives.

"She can come out of hiding."

The words left his mouth and hung in the air between Ben and Isaac.

"That's what I'm thinking." Isaac leaned against the desk. "If she contacts you and you need my help with anything, just say so. You know that Lizzy and I think the world of Sadie."

Ben was already shaking his head. "It doesn't matter, Isaac. Unless she joins the Amish church, we could never be together. I am grateful that she is free to come home, though. More than anything, I want her to be safe and happy. I have prayed to *Gott* every day for Him to bless her and let her come home."

"He listened."

Sadie.

Ben stood so fast he knocked over the chair that he had been working on. He never even glanced at it. All his focus was on the lovely woman standing inside the door. His heart sped up and his mouth went dry.

She was dressed Plain. He'd never seen anything lovelier than Sadie standing in his workshop wearing a heavy black cape, and under it he could see she had on a rose-colored Amish dress and plain brown boots. On her head, a crisp white prayer *kapp* covered most of her hair. She was holding a black bonnet.

In short, she looked like an Amish woman and not like the *Englisch* woman who had landed in his life so unexpectedly all those months ago. His chest grew tight and his breathing was constricted. Hope flared in his soul, but he struggled to keep it under control. If she wasn't here to stay, or if she wasn't part of the Amish world now, he didn't want the knowledge to crush him.

"Sadie—" he began and stopped, unsure what to start with. So many thoughts were colliding inside him, his mind was having trouble sorting them all out. All he could do was stare at the woman who had stolen his heart, half fearing that she would disappear if he blinked.

"I will see you later, my friend." Isaac placed a hand briefly on his shoulder, wordlessly imparting his support. Ben started. He had forgotten the other man was standing next to him, he'd been so focused on Sadie.

Apologetically, he smiled at Isaac. "Sure. I will see you later."

"Sadie," Isaac murmured as he moved past her. "It's good to see you."

"Same goes, Isaac," she replied, shooting him a tight smile. Ben could see the apprehension in it. She was as nervous as he was.

Some of his own anxiety dwindled as the urge to reassure her inserted itself.

"I read the article your brother wrote in the paper. Are you out of danger now?" It might have seemed obvious, but he needed to know that she was safe.

"Completely," she whispered. She took a step closer and halted. "The men who were after us are now all out of commission. I was given the news a month ago."

Wait. A month ago? Some of his hope died. If she had waited a month before contacting him... But what about her clothing?

"I'm confused," he admitted. "If you are safe, and have been for a month—"

"Why am I only coming here now?" She completed his sentence. He shrugged. After everything they'd been through together, it seemed to him that he deserved some answers.

"I needed time, Ben. Time to put my stuff in order, time to cut my ties."

"Cut your ties?" He advanced a step toward her. That sounded positive.

"Yes." Her caramel-brown eyes, the eyes that had snared him from the first day, met his. "I needed to cut most of my ties with the *Englisch* world. I have talked with the bishop here. Several times, in fact. He remembered my father and mother. He wanted me to wait until I was sure that I wanted to be Amish before I spoke with you. It was the hardest thing to not run to you the moment I was free, but I knew I had to obey him."

She had been thinking of him. Another step. The distance between them was shrinking. "You have made your decision."

A laugh trickled gently from her lips. "You can look at the way I'm dressed and ask? Yes, I have made my choice."

She took the final step and was suddenly only inches away from him. Her hand lifted and touched his cheek. "Ben, I remember us. As we were as children, and as we are now. There has always been a bond between us, hasn't there? Even when I couldn't remember, I felt that connection."

His hand covered hers where it rested, warm and smooth against his face. "You were my best friend when we were children. I lost so much the day you left. I, too, have sensed this connection."

He lifted her hand from his face but didn't let go. They stood, holding hands, staring into each other's eyes.

"I'm not Amish yet," she said. "The bishop has asked me to continue to meet with him until he feels I'm ready to join the church. I'd do it today if he agreed."

"You know, the moment he agrees, I'm going to ask you to be my wife."

The smile that hovered about her lips burst forth and became a grin. "I hope so. And you know, the moment you ask me to be your wife, I will say yes."

His heart was so full, he found himself needing a second. Her eyes were bright and glistening.

"I love you, Sadie Ann. With all my heart. I want you to be a part of my and Nathaniel's life for the rest of our days." It was as close to a proposal as he could go, but he was at peace, knowing that soon he'd be making a true proposal. Then, during the harvest season, he'd make her his bride.

She sighed, a happy sound that filled all the empty corners in his lonely heart. "I love you, too, Ben. I can't wait until you can ask me to be your wife."

He leaned forward and gently, tenderly, touched her forehead with his lips.

"What about your brother?" He had to ask.

"He knows everything and is happy for me. He'll miss me, of course. But we will stay in touch. Even if I was born here, Kurt is and always will be my brother. The bishop told me that he doesn't have a problem with Kurt visiting now and again. Although I have a feeling that Kurt will be busy with his career for a while.

His new boss was very impressed with his work on the illegal human trafficking articles."

He was glad. He would always think of Kurt as a friend. Having him as a brother-in-law would please him, as well.

They left the shop together and headed toward his home. The ground was covered with a fresh layer of snow, and the March air was frigid. He didn't mind. His entire being seemed to be suffused with warmth from the joy of having his love by his side again. He wanted to jump and shout his feelings aloud, he could almost burst with how blessed he was.

He did nothing of the sort, of course. Instead, he and Sadie walked sedately side by side, murmuring softly, making plans for the upcoming months. They might not be officially engaged yet, but he knew that they had already promised themselves to each other.

The front screen door banged open, interrupting their quiet conversation. Sadie laughed as Nathaniel charged out the door and literally threw himself off the porch before running into her arms.

"Sadie! You came back! *Dat*, Sadie *es cumme*!"

A wide grin flashed across Ben's face as Sadie embraced his exuberant son tightly. "*Jah*, I can see that she is home. Are you *gut* with that?"

There was a bit of playfulness in the question. He could see that his son was overjoyed.

"*Jah!* I am happy!" Nathaniel pulled back to look up into Sadie's face. "I prayed and prayed that *Gott* would bring you back. Are you going to be my new *mamm*?"

Both Sadie and Ben flushed at the innocent question.

"Easy, son. She just came back to us. She needs to join the church before we can talk about that."

Sadie raised her eyebrows at him. He bit back a smile of understanding. They had talked about nothing but that for the past twenty minutes. But he knew it wouldn't be proper to say anything to Nathaniel yet.

But soon, he promised himself, looking into her beloved face, soon they would marry and become a family.

Later that afternoon, he walked her back to her *grossmamma's haus* where she would live until they were wed. He hesitated to leave her. It seemed cruel that he had her back and had to leave her again. He said as much.

"Only until tomorrow, dear Ben." She reached out and touched his hand.

He leaned forward and kissed her, barely a whisper across her soft lips. "Until tomorrow, my dear one."

And all the days that followed.

EPILOGUE

"*Mamm*, when will baby Evie be able to play with me?" Nathaniel asked.

Ben grinned at Sadie and waited for her to answer the question. Sadie bit her lip, holding back her returning smile. She was very careful not to give the impression that she was laughing at Nathaniel. At eight and a half, he thought he was quite grown-up. Ben knew that Sadie wasn't laughing at Nathaniel, she just thought he was adorable. Plus, whenever he called her *mamm*, her heart just about melted right out of her chest.

She was so blessed with her men.

And now she had another wee blessing.

Cuddling her sleeping daughter closer in her arms, she smoothed a kiss on the tiny forehead. Sometimes she had to remind herself to breathe, her happiness was so overwhelming.

She thought about the months following the arrests of Ethan Nettle and his son. They had both been convicted, and with the list of crimes against them, they would spend the rest of their lives in prison. Jeffrey was free, and although still bitter, he had told her that he never blamed her. In fact, he said that he would have intervened if he'd seen her getting kidnapped. Ironically, that meant he would have been the one who died that day.

"You're the same age as my baby sister. I couldn't have stood by and done nothing," he'd said.

She prayed for him every day.

She returned her attention to Nathaniel, who was watching her with avid eyes.

"Nathaniel, she won't be able to play with you for a while yet. She's only five days old."

He scrunched up his face and peered at his new sister with disgust. He'd been hoping that she would be able to play immediately, she was certain of it. Evelyn yawned and grunted and stretched in her sleep. Stepping so that he was leaning against his stepmother, Nathaniel placed a very gentle finger in one of the small fists. When Evelyn grabbed his finger and held on tight in her sleep, his scowl softened. Something akin to awe glowed on his features.

"She ain't a boy, and she can't do anything," he announced to his parents. "Still, I guess she's fine, as far as babies go."

Sadie and Ben both chuckled. Her eyes lifted to meet his. The love she saw reflected in his gaze warmed her. Evelyn stretched again, her mouth moving in smacking movements. Someone was hungry. Ben laughed again, bending to kiss his wife.

"Oh, yuck. Kissing." Nathaniel sighed, positively disgusted with the behavior of his parents. Sadie bit back another laugh, not wanting to hurt his feelings.

"Come, Nathaniel," Ben said, standing. "I could use your help in the barn for a bit."

Nathaniel kissed his sister and waved at Sadie before following his father out to the barn. Alone, Sadie fed the newborn and then put her down in her bassinet to sleep. Hearing voices when she returned to the kitchen area, Sadie peered out the open window, breathing in the sweet-scented spring air. She loved this time of year, with all the blossoms and flowers blooming.

Ah, Isaac had arrived. It was good to see that his friendship with Ben had grown solid and strong, like when they had all been children together. Her memories of her past had returned. Sadie recalled many times when she had followed Ben and Isaac around. Those were happy memories. The dark memories, the ones of her father's death and the period after that, were harder. Between those memories and her near brush with death, she'd suffered from several months of nightmares, and even some anxiety. Thankfully, those had faded since she joined the Amish church and married Ben.

Isaac's wife, Lizzy, was walking toward the house. Sadie threw the door open and moved out onto the porch, not even bothering with shoes.

"Lizzy, it is wonderful to see you. I didn't know that you were coming over to visit."

"Ack, of course I was coming. The minute I knew my husband was coming to see Ben, I knew that I would come and spend time with my dearest friend."

Joy filled Sadie with its warmth. She felt as though she were standing in her own patch of sunlight. She wanted to pinch herself to assure herself that she was truly awake. But she knew she was. God had brought her through the storm and the trials and had blessed her with friends who would stand by her and a man and children who would love her all the days that God had allotted them on His earth.

She was overwhelmed by the blessings she had been given so freely, her heart was near to bursting.

"God is so good," she murmured.

"*Jah, Gott* is very *gut.*" Lizzy gave her an understanding smile. Sadie gestured for Lizzy to come inside. As the woman moved past her to enter the house, Sadie's smile widened. Lizzy hadn't said anything, as most Amish women did not speak of such things to anyone beyond their husbands, but even in her Amish attire, it appeared that her friend might be expecting. She hoped so. She knew that Lizzy and Isaac wanted a child. She mentally said a prayer that God would bless them with a large family.

Lizzy caught her glance and laid a hand on her midsection. Although she didn't say anything, her blazing smile and nod confirmed Sadie's suspicions. One more joy to pile on top of all the other sources of happiness in her life. "God is good, indeed," she repeated.

That night, after their guests had left and the children had been put to bed, Ben draped Sadie's cloak around her shoulders and led her out to the front porch. They sat close together on the porch swing he had made her as a wedding gift. She snuggled close to her husband, inhaling the combined scents of the soap she had made and the night air and was content.

"I think Isaac and Lizzy are going to have a child," she said softly.

He kissed the top of her head. With his foot, he gave a small push against the porch floor to make the swing sway gently. "*Jah*, I think so, too. It is *gut*."

"I received a letter from Kurt today."

"*Jah?* What did our brother write?"

She loved hearing him claim kinship with Kurt. "He said he has a new assignment that will take him out of the area for a bit, he couldn't say what, but I think he was excited. His handwriting was a bit harder to read. Anyway, he wants to come and stay with us for a few days before he leaves."

"He is always welcome." Ben looked up at the stars for a moment. "You know, I will always have a warm spot in my heart for him. It is because of him that we were reunited."

She turned to her husband. "I feel the same. I love you so much, Ben Mast. You and our children have filled all the empty spaces in my heart."

His eyes bright, Ben leaned closer and kissed her. Sadie allowed her eyes to close as she praised her God for His faithful care.

When the kiss ended, she rested her head against her husband, knowing she was where she belonged.

* * * * *

*If you enjoyed this book, don't miss the other
heart-stopping Amish adventures from
Dana R. Lynn's Amish Country Justice series:*

Plain Target
Plain Retribution
Amish Christmas Abduction
Amish Country Ambush
Amish Christmas Emergency
Guarding the Amish Midwife

Find more great reads at www.LoveInspired.com.

Dear Reader,

I am so thrilled to be able to tell you another story from Waylan Grove, Ohio. Sadie, Ben and Nathaniel are all brand-new characters. I fell in love with them as I wrote this book, and I hope you did, too.

I have always been intrigued by the idea of amnesia. When Sadie woke up to discover she had no memories and a killer after her, it took a lot of determination to survive and find the truth. Sadie had those qualities. What she lacked, though, was faith.

Ben Mast has survived a horrible heartbreak. He has been wounded, but somehow his faith has remained strong. I loved watching him show Sadie the truths about God while they fell in love and tried to escape a killer.

Thank you for reading *Hidden in Amish Country*. I love to connect with readers. You can find me on Facebook, Twitter and Instagram. Or contact me through my website, www.danarlynn.com.

Blessings,
Dana R. Lynn

Get 4 FREE REWARDS!

We'll send you 2 FREE Books plus 2 FREE Mystery Gifts.

Love Inspired® Suspense books feature Christian characters facing challenges to their faith... and lives.

FREE Value Over $20

YES! Please send me 2 FREE Love Inspired® Suspense novels and my 2 FREE mystery gifts (gifts are worth about $10 retail). After receiving them, if I don't wish to receive any more books, I can return the shipping statement marked "cancel." If I don't cancel, I will receive 6 brand-new novels every month and be billed just $5.24 each for the regular-print edition or $5.99 each for the larger-print edition in the U.S., or $5.74 each for the regular-print edition or $6.24 each for the larger-print edition in Canada. That's a savings of at least 13% off the cover price. It's quite a bargain! Shipping and handling is just 50¢ per book in the U.S. and $1.25 per book in Canada.* I understand that accepting the 2 free books and gifts places me under no obligation to buy anything. I can always return a shipment and cancel at any time. The free books and gifts are mine to keep no matter what I decide.

Choose one: ☐ **Love Inspired® Suspense Regular-Print** (153/353 IDN GNWN)   ☐ **Love Inspired® Suspense Larger-Print** (107/307 IDN GNWN)

Name (please print)

Address   Apt. #

City   State/Province   Zip/Postal Code

Mail to the **Reader Service:**
IN U.S.A.: P.O. Box 1341, Buffalo, NY 14240-8531
IN CANADA: P.O. Box 603, Fort Erie, Ontario L2A 5X3

Want to try 2 free books from another series? Call 1-800-873-8635 or visit www.ReaderService.com.

SPECIAL EXCERPT FROM

SUSPENSE

*An NYPD officer's widow becomes the target of
her husband's killer. Can her husband's best friend
and his K-9 partner keep her safe and take the
murderer down once and for all?*

Read on for a sneak preview of
Sworn to Protect *by Shirlee McCoy,*
the exciting conclusion to the
True Blue K-9 Unit *series, available*
November 2019 from Love Inspired Suspense.

"Come in," Katie Jameson called, bracing herself for the meeting with Dr. Ritter.

The door swung open and a man in a white lab coat stepped in, holding her chart close to his face.

Only, he was not the doctor she was expecting.

Dr. Ritter was in his early sixties with salt-and-pepper hair and enough extra weight to fill out his lab coat. The doctor who was moving toward her had dark hair and a muscular build. His scuffed shoes and baggy lab coat made her wonder if he were a resident at the hospital where she would be giving birth.

"Good morning," she said. She had been meeting with Dr. Ritter since the beginning of the pregnancy. He understood her feelings about the birth. Talking about the fact that Jordan wouldn't be around for his daughter's birth, her childhood, her life always brought her close to the tears she despised.

"Morning," he mumbled.

"Is Dr. Ritter running late?" she asked, uneasiness joining the unsettled feeling in the pit of her stomach.

"He won't be able to make it," the man said, lowering the charts and grinning.

She went cold with terror.

She knew the hazel eyes, the lopsided grin, the high forehead. "Martin," she stammered.

"Sorry it took me so long to get to you, sweetheart. I had to watch from a distance until I was certain we could be alone."

"Watch?"

"They wanted to keep me in the hospital, but our love is too strong to be denied. I escaped for you. For us." He lifted a hand, and if she had not jerked back, his fingers would have brushed her cheek.

He scowled. "Have they brainwashed you? Have they turned you against me?"

"You did that yourself when you murdered my husband," she responded.

Don't miss
Sworn to Protect *by Shirlee McCoy,*
available November 2019 wherever
Love Inspired® Suspense books and ebooks are sold.

www.LoveInspired.com

*Surprise fatherhood, Southern charm and a
heartwarming family Christmas—read on for a sneak
peek at* Low Country Christmas, *the conclusion to
Lee Tobin McClain's Safe Haven series!*

Cash remembered coming out to Ma Dixie's place at Christmas time growing up. The contrast with his own foster family's home had been extreme. There, six themed Christmas trees were spread throughout the house, decorated perfectly by the commercial operation that brought them out each year and took them away after the holidays. That same company had wrapped garlands around the staircase and strung lights outside the house.

It had all been grand. He remembered being shocked and impressed his first year with the family, because it had been so different from the humble holidays back in Alabama. But he hadn't been allowed to invite his brothers over; too much noise and mess, his foster mother had always said. If he wanted to see them, he had to find a ride out to Ma Dixie's, which he had done frequently.

Here, Christmas really felt like Christmas.

He opened another box of ornaments, pulled out an angel made of hard plastic and handed it to Holly to place on the tree.

"Is this your tree topper, Ma?" Holly asked, holding it up.

"Yes, it is. I usually have Pudge put it up, but…could you do it, Cash, honey?"

He did, easily reaching the top of the small tree. "Is Pudge okay?" he asked Ma. "Is that why the place isn't decorated yet? He's too sick to help?"

Ma arranged the last figures in the Nativity scene and sank down onto the couch. "That's part of it. Mostly, it's me feeling blue. I'm not used to Christmas with no kids around."

Holly tilted her head to one side. "Did you have a lot of kids?"

"Dozens," Ma said with a wide smile. "That's the beauty of being a foster parent."

"Oh," Holly said as she sank down onto an ottoman beside Ma. "Do you…not foster anymore?"

Ma sighed. "I really can't with Pudge having all these doctor appointments. I guess maybe we're getting too old for it." She looked wistfully at the tree. "I just, you know, always enjoyed having the little ones around."

Holly looked thoughtful. "Is that why you wanted to take care of Penny? Not to help me out, but to have a little one around?"

"That's part of it," Ma said, "but don't you worry about it. I understand being picky where your child is concerned."

"It's not pickiness," Holly said. "If I were being picky, who better than an experienced foster parent like you?" She reached out and rubbed Ma's arm back and forth, two or three times, an affectionate gesture that made Ma smile.

Cash came over and sat at Holly's side, leaning against the ottoman. His heart, like that of the Grinch in the movie playing muted on the television, seemed to be expanding.

He'd taken plenty of women to high-end Christmas parties and fancy restaurants. But sitting here in Ma Dixie's house, talking with her about holidays and kids and family problems, decorating the tree with her, felt different. Like coming home.

Like coming home, with Holly beside him.

He put that feeling together with the questions his brother and Pudge had been asking. He was getting the horrifying notion that he might be falling in love with Holly. But he wasn't the falling-in-love type, or the settling-down type. And Holly wasn't the type for a short, superficial fling.

So what exactly was he going to do with all these feelings?

Don't miss Lee Tobin McClain's
Low Country Christmas,
available October 2019 from HQN Books!